# A Nigh

Carter felt the woman's arms leave his back for a second or two and decided to roll her over on top of him. Part way through the change of position, a searing pain tore at him as a blade entered his lower back. The breath torn from his lungs by shock and pain, he reached with his left hand, caught her knife hand by the wrist, and twisted until he heard bone snap. As he leaned back, the room spun. The knife still sticking from his back, he eased himself from her, disengaging flesh from flesh in what was no longer a sex act....

# NICK CARTER IS IT!

# FROM THE NICK CARTER
## KILLMASTER SERIES

ARCTIC ABDUCTION

# KILL MASTER
# NICK CARTER

J

JOVE BOOKS, NEW YORK

KILLMASTER #260: ARCTIC ABDUCTION

A Jove Book / published by arrangement with
The Condé Nast Publications, Inc.

PRINTING HISTORY
Jove edition / April 1990

ISBN: 0-515-10292-X

Jove Books are published by The Berkley Publishing Group,
200 Madison Avenue, New York, New York 10016.
The name "JOVE" and the "J" logo
are trademarks belonging to Jove Publications, Inc.

PRINTED IN THE UNITED STATES OF AMERICA

10  9  8  7  6  5  4  3  2  1

*Dedicated to the men and women of the
Secret Services of the United States of America*

# PROLOGUE

*June*
*Bristol Bay, Alaska*

The sea had finally calmed and fishermen were leaving their wooden shacks to check on the damage to their fishing boats. The storm had been the worst to come pouring out of the Bering Sea in a decade. The last time they'd seen black clouds roiling in so fast, backed up with winds up to a hundred miles an hour, they'd lost half their fleet and their nets took weeks to repair.

The rain was still coming down in sheets but the wind had died down. The breakers, born from twenty-five-foot waves, had receded to a strong chop. Danger still lurked outside their homes, but the men couldn't wait. The boats were their life. They had to find out if they still had jobs, if their children would have food in the months to come.

They came as if on signal, one after the other, to the still boiling shore, and what they found they would never forget as long as they lived. It wasn't the boats. They had expected damage. But among the splintered shells that had once been boats, the limp bodies of children, teen-agers mostly, washed to and fro in the chop, or hung, impaled from long splinters of wood, their bodies white, defenseless against the angry sea.

When the wind finally died, helicopters from the Coast Guard station at Anchorage came in ones and twos, and took the shattered bodies away in black plastic bags. The men stood around, their wives and children confined to their houses. They looked at each other with eyes that had seen too much death, and they wept. They wept for torn bodies, white and bloated, twenty children that might have been their own.

They wiped away their tears with rough woollen sleeves and turned to the boats. Their own losses seemed petty now. Boats could be replaced. Nets could be mended. But the crushed and shattered bodies of children could never be anything but what they were, lost futures, symbols of what might have been but would never be.

At Anchorage the chief of surgery at Anchorage General walked with the coroner from one dissection table to the next examining the bodies. They had been stripped naked, the pitiful remains of their clothes piled, some still wet, at the bottom of each table.

"The chief of police has sent fingerprints and hair samples to Washington," the chief of surgery said, wearily combing his fingers through his salt-and-pepper hair.

"Where the hell did they come from?" the coroner asked, as if speaking to himself. "No reports of missing kids were made. No one has come forward to claim them."

"I don't know," the chief of surgery said. "I just don't know."

# ONE

*January*
*Washington, D.C.*

Nick Carter parked his classic racing-green Jaguar XKE around the corner from the Jefferson Hotel and the National Geographic Society headquarters, and walked to the embassy of the Union of Soviet Socialist Republics. It was a crisp winter night, cloudless, the smell of the city fresh after a powdery coating of new snow. The minute flakes were banked in places, disturbed by an earlier breeze. They lined his path as he walked along 16th Street to the embassy entrance, snow crunching under patent leather shoes.

Limousines pulled up to the huge portico in a long stream, disgorging men and women from the upper echelons of government and society. The process was slow. Soviet security checked out every guest carefully while others waited patiently. They had all played the game before.

Carter presented his invitation, submitted to an electronic search, and left his coat at a checkroom near the entrance. He walked casually through the huge vestibule

3

to the ballroom, then headed for the bar at the far end. In his tuxedo, complete with black tie, his above-average height and rugged good looks attracted the attention of both seasoned and novice Capitol Hill females. He ignored the admiring glances cast his way, and managed to get the attention of a bartender.

The men behind the long table were alike in one respect: they were professionals as he was, KGB as part of the background. While he was being served, the barman's eyes held his for a moment and a signal passed between them. Instinct born out of years of training and fieldwork identified men of the same stripe. Carter accepted a scotch and headed for the reception line. It was not his intent to join the line, but to observe from a distance. The fact that he was in the Soviet Embassy was, in itself, an uncommon event. He'd been closeted with David Hawk and Rupert Smith for a good part of the afternoon examining Soviet motives for issuing an invitation to him . . .

"It bothers me that they know enough about you to send an invitation," Smith had commented. Rupert Smith was head of Operations at AXE, an ultrasecret agency headed by Hawk, formed many years earlier at the request of the president. "And to hand deliver it to your door. It doesn't leave much doubt about their knowledge of you."

"I don't like it. We've run into people who've known of you on assignments, but not here, not so blatantly," Hawk said, pacing his office, leaving in his wake a stream of foul-smelling blue-gray smoke from the ever-present cigar. He was shorter than Carter by a head, and older. He wore conservative dark suits, and his abundant white hair had a mind of its own. The fact that he frequently ran stubby fingers through it didn't help. "You'll have to sell the brownstone in Georgetown, Nick," he went on. "In the meantime you can use our safe house on New York Avenue."

"That's just great," Carter said, hating to lose the first real home he'd had in years. "What do you think they want?" he asked, lighting a cigarette with a gold Dunhill lighter.

"There's no way we can answer that question," Smith replied. "It's something you'll have to learn for yourself. We'll have people on you, of course."

Their conversation had covered all possible scenarios and they hadn't come up with the answer, so here he was, standing in the ballroom of the Soviet embassy, watching people enter and meet the ambassador and his wife.

"Are you as bored as I am?" a female voice behind him asked. The voice had a rich tone to it that promised a face and a body to match. An amateur Henry Higgins, Carter could recognize the regional accents of most Americans. This one was a puzzler, but when he turned to her, the face and body exceeded his expectations. She had high cheekbones, an olive complexion, huge brown eyes with long eyelashes, and glossy, almost blue-black hair. She was wearing a strapless light green silk sheath, a wisp of matching fabric draped around her shoulders. Her mouth was red and moist, perfectly formed. He found the urge to kiss her almost irresistible, even in the embassy crowd. He hoped that her effect on his libido was not evident to anyone but himself—and her.

"Hard to judge. I've just arrived," he said. The thought occurred that she must have been watching him to single him out for the question.

Why did everyone have to have a motive? he asked himself. She was the best-looking woman in the room and didn't appear to be with anyone. "Even if someone says only a few words, I'm usually good at guessing where he or she is from," he told her. "But you're a mystery."

"I'm not surprised," she said, looking at him over her champagne glass with those dark eyes. He found he couldn't stop staring at them. Flecks of gray, spread out like a sunburst from her pupils, gave them a unique color mixture he'd never seen. "I was born on Kodiak Island," she went on. "But my father was in the military and he was shipped all over the States and overseas."

"My name is Carter. Nick Carter," he said, offering a hand.

She took it and held it as if to possess it for some time. Her grip was firm, her hand not as soft as he'd expected. All the while she held his eyes with hers, an enigmatic smile on her face, almost mocking, certainly challenging. "I'm Nancy Bell," she said, the expression changing to a warm smile that lit up the space around her. "Associate librarian with the Library of Congress. Bored associate at the moment."

A woman as stunning as Nancy Bell couldn't be bored at such a function, Carter mused. If she were not with him, she would be surrounded by a half-dozen fawning men. So what was she doing here?

"And what does a Nick Carter do?" she asked, her mouth ending in a pout, an affectation she obviously thought endearing.

"I'm with Amalgamated Press and Wire Services. Mostly overseas work. I rarely get to see bashes like this."

"Washington's loss," she murmured. Then she added, "As a what, foreign correspondent?"

"You might say that." He watched her for reactions

but saw nothing unusual. Then one thing struck him: she wasn't casing the room as most beautiful women would. She concentrated on him. Nothing else was happening to him at the reception, so he went along with her play. "Go with the flow," Rupert Smith had suggested. So he'd go with the flow.

"If you're so bored, why come?" he asked.

"Because to stay home alone would be worse. Coming here, at least a girl can meet a Nick Carter."

She didn't learn that in Kodiak, he told himself.

"I don't suppose there'll be dancing later?" he asked.

"You don't suppose exactly right," she said, laughing low in her throat. When she laughed, her full breasts came alive.

The problem was, Carter didn't know the game. He figured his odds at fifty-fifty. If he stayed with her, he'd either be doing the right thing or he'd be missing the contact that might follow from some other source. But if he did hang around with Nancy Bell, he'd probably have one hell of an evening.

He decided to compromise, or at least delay the inevitable. "Why don't we freshen our drinks and you take me on a tour of this place? I've never seen all of it before."

"And you won't see all of it now," she said, then placed an index finger on his chin. "Why do I feel that I'm being held in reserve while the handsome male looks over the field?"

It was his turn to laugh, which he did, dutifully. Smitty said he had people on him here. Maybe one of them would get to him with some intelligence. Maybe someone would see him with the woman and realize he would probably leave early. He'd do the rounds, use the men's room for a last possible contact, then decide what to do.

• • •

On the street a half hour later, he walked to his car and drove it to the embassy steps. Nancy waited under the portico in a fox fur coat. Carter helped her into the low-slung seat. He'd told her he was with Amalgamated Press and Wire Services, the front for AXE, and now she would know his car. So be it. If they, whoever they were, knew where he lived, he'd have to go along until he knew what the bottom line was going to be. He'd played this game all too many times. Maybe by leaving himself open, he could get to the source and eliminate the problem. Elimination was his game. Carter's AXE code was Killmaster N3, licensed to kill when the job warranted termination.

They danced at the Washington Hilton and Towers, sat over a cognac at the piano bar, and left when her liquid eyes were sending messages that he was unable to ignore.

He tried to think of her as the reason for his invitation by the Soviets but found this difficult to believe. They had talked a great deal before they both felt the heat build in them and she'd revealed a great deal about herself. She was either the best actress in the world, a true innocent, or as slick an agent as he'd met.

They drove to her apartment in Columbia Heights. While she changed into "something more comfortable," he searched the apartment except for her bedroom and found nothing suspicious.

When she returned in a loosely belted Japanese-style robe, he took her in his arms and kissed her, long and with great passion, until her knees buckled. He picked her up and carried her to the sofa, then made an excuse to go to the john that had a door leading into her bedroom. While in her room, he ran his hands under the pillows and under the mattress along both sides in search of a weapon. He was just returning when he encountered her on her way in to see what was keeping him.

He'd found nothing. No one else had contacted him, not even one of his own. So this had to be an innocent encounter. The damned job had made him totally paranoid, he thought. A beautiful woman like this for the asking and he was searching her bedroom as if she were KGB and setting him up.

He made an about-face in attitude in seconds and easily lifted her and deposited her on the bed. They clutched at each other, a madness upon them that had been growing all evening. He possessed her mouth while a hand pulled the silken material from her shoulders.

She wouldn't release his mouth while she desperately tried to get her hands past buttons and zippers to the flesh of the man she'd chosen for the night.

Naked and bound together from mouth to toe, they rolled across the bed, she ascending at times, he at others. She tore her mouth away and moaned that she couldn't stand to wait another second. She pulled him on her and opened her legs to him.

He entered her and his excitement mounted as he felt the furnacelike heat of her body. Gone was all suspicion, all his foolish searching for motivation. All he could think of was the woman who screamed out for satisfaction and the sensation he felt bound to supply. In the process, he felt himself peaking and tried to slow down the action to give her total fulfillment. He felt her arms leave his back for a second or two and decided to roll her over on top of him. Partway through the change of position, a searing pain tore at the triceps of his right arm and a blade entered his lower back.

The pain was excruciating as the blade was plunged

to the hilt. The breath torn from his lungs by shock and pain, he reached with his left hand, caught her knife hand by the wrist, and twisted until he heard bone snap. She was looking up at him, a scream forming at the back of her throat, her expression one of total surprise. In the fraction of a second he observed her shock, he realized that in his decision to move, the back of his arm, had changed the path of her thrust. He learned back, blood pouring from his arm, the knife sticking from his back. He supported his weight with the bloody right hand and smashed her face as hard as he could with his left fist. He felt bone snap. Her head rolled to one side.

Carter felt himself getting dizzy. The room spun as he eased himself from her, disengaging flesh from flesh in what was no longer a sex act. Carter almost fell to the floor, the hilt of the knife close to the carpet, the move almost causing further penetration, but he managed to save himself with his good arm and crawl to the phone.

With his bloody right hand, the fingers numb, he pulsed in seven digits that would tell the AXE computer that he was in trouble. The synthesized voice sounded sympathetic when it responded.

"What is it, N3?"

"I'm at the... Columbia Apartments... on Eleventh Street. Apartment Twelve-sixteen. I've been... stabbed. Send our people," he said before the room began to spin once more. He slid sideways to the floor and into a black void.

# TWO

In a two-story building built for function rather than beauty on the grounds of AXE's secret facility in the seclusion of the Virginia hills not far from Washington and Langley, Hawk sat beside Carter's bed. Rupert Smith was with him and Howard Schmidt, their resident expert on identification and gadgets. A staff doctor stood over the bed, one of Carter's hands in a meaty paw. The medic had been repairing AXE agents, returned from duty in bad shape, from the time years earlier when Hawk had set up the Virginia facility for training and recuperation.

"He's coming around," the doctor announced.

Carter was looking at them calmly. His expression showed immediate recognition. He appeared to be alert from the beginning. "So how did I blow it?" he asked.

"We blew it. This wasn't exactly a solo act," Hawk growled. "I had four men and two women on you all the time. We couldn't do much when you entered her apartment, but by then we figured she was not one of them."

"How did she do it? I searched her place thoroughly."

11

"Damned ingenious." Schmidt spoke for the first time. "She had the knife taped lightly to the back of her right leg. It was flesh-colored and she'd used pancake makeup to camouflage it further."

"The back of her leg. Christ," Carter grunted. "That's one of the last places you'd be likely to find it in a first encounter."

"Not exactly our area of expertise," Hawk commented dryly. "We've got her here, in the next room."

"Did you question her yet?"

"No. We thought you might help," the doctor said. "She's got a broken wrist and loose bone fragments around her third and fourth cervical vertebrae, minute but temporarily painful. It's lucky you didn't shatter her jaw or we'd never get her to talk."

"When do we do it?" Carter asked.

"Tomorrow," the doctor answered. "You were damned lucky, Nick. The arm wound is superficial and the knife didn't do any major damage—sliced into the liver but didn't touch major arteries or veins. Bed rest for you for a couple of weeks to make sure it mends. Damned tricky organ, the liver. Can't fool around with it."

"Who do you think she is?" Carter asked his boss.

"She's one of theirs, no doubt. What did she tell you?"

"Innocent as a lamb. Born in Alaska, Kodiak. Educated in the East as a librarian. Works at the Library of Congress."

"All lies, of course," Smith contributed. "She just had to be with you once."

"We've lost a few highly placed scientific and military men to ladies like her. We find them in apartments that were rented by the month,'' Hawk said. ''Female hit men.''

''To quote my own texts,'' Schmidt interjected: *''The Executive Action Department, Department Five, is a group the KGB keeps most secret. Responsible for the Soviet Union's political murders, kidnappings, and sabotage. They call it* mokrie dela, *or 'wet affairs.'''*

''But she was as American as the proverbial apple pie,'' Carter said. ''I know they have schools over there where their agents live in communities set up as American towns, but she was too good for that. Maybe a recruit?''

''We'll know tomorrow,'' Schmidt said. ''I've just completed tests on a new truth drug, you'll be pleased to know. Works faster than the one I've supplied you with recently, Nick. And it has no side effects. I've never seen it fail.''

''I'm looking forward to it,'' Carter said, closing his eyes. As he drifted off to sleep, he could still hear the voices of friends drone on but the words soon faded.

''Let's leave him,'' the doctor suggested. ''I'll be in my office if you need me.''

Hawk led the way to a lounge and poured himself a cup of coffee from a Mr. Coffee on a table by the far wall. The whole installation was secure. They could talk freely. ''I'm worried about this one,'' he said, taking a sip from the steaming brew. ''Damned blatant operation. The Soviets send an invitation to our best agent to what looked like an innocent reception. They're not supposed to know where he lives, but the invitation was delivered to his house in Georgetown. They target him to be taken from their own embassy and killed by one of their people. Doesn't make sense.''

''So maybe it's not the Soviets,'' Smith offered. ''If

it had worked, the Soviets would have looked bad. No one expected the woman to be caught."

"We've got enough enemies. It could have been anyone. Even the invitation could have been phony," Schmidt said.

Hawk left his coffee and paced the room. He was a noted pacer. His office at Dupont Circle, AXE headquarters, was usually filled with cigar smoke, and as he moved about the room, his head disturbed the blue-gray cloud that hovered over him. Today he didn't smoke. He rarely smoked at the training facility and never in the hospital. "Could be disinformation—reverse psychology—could be anything," he muttered while he walked. "At least we have the girl and tomorrow we'll know who she is. If she's one of theirs, they've pulled a major blunder."

"If she's the one who killed off the others, they had every reason to expect success," Smith offered.

"But the invitation was so blatant," Schmidt said, shaking his head.

"If everything had gone according to plan, we'd have lost Nick and we'd never be sure where the invitation came from," Hawk said, pouring the cold coffee down a sink in the far corner and rinsing the mug. "Let's leave it until tomorrow."

In the huge, relatively new Soviet embassy on 16th Street, the ambassador, Sergei Alexandrovich Lubkov, sat behind the desk in his office, still dressed in the formal clothes he'd worn the night before. A bottle of vodka sat in front of him. A smudged glass sitting on the desk organizer rested amid a dozen rings where moisture had collected as the glass had been used and replaced through the long hours of the night.

Across from the ambassador sat two men, each with his black bow tie undone and askew, his collar loosened, and his tuxedo jacket thrown over the back of his chair. Each man, his face grim, needed a shave. Both also needed some sleep and some relief from the constant criticism of the man who represented the Union of Soviet Socialist Republics in Washington.

One man, Anatoly Pavli Morotov, smaller than the other two and thin to the point of emaciation, was with the First Chief Directorate, First Department, the group who were responsible for KGB activity in Canada and the United States. The largest of the three, Yuri Ivanovich Tsarev, a giant of a man with arms and legs like tree trunks and a head that looked like an unworked chunk of granite, sat with his massive head bowed. The blunder was his responsibility. The penalty could be a life of isolation and horror if the damage could not be salvaged.

"I've got to wire your chief in the next hour or two," the ambassador said, his voice projecting his fatigue. "What am I going to tell him? You have jeopardized the First Minister's pet project. His fury will be monumental."

"We can't be sure of that," Morotov said. He was in charge of all KGB activity east of the Mississippi in the States and Winnipeg in Canada. "The girl has disappeared. She might be dead. We have no way of knowing."

"Don't be a fool, Anatoly Pavli," Lubkov snapped. "Her apartment is empty. Her car is gone."

"We cannot be sure she is in their hands," Tsarev insisted for the tenth time that night. "She is our best. She had never failed in the past. I assume she will call in within the next few hours."

The ambassador moved from his chair and walked to

the window. A light snow was falling. It reminded him of home. "Well, I cannot wait, or all our necks are in the noose," he warned. "They probably are anyway. I must assume the worst." He threw open the window to clear the room of smoke and the smell of fear. "Damn your stupidity, Tsarev! The whole idea was insane. I should never have let you talk me into it."

"If it had worked, we'd have been immortalized in the intelligence community," Tsarev said. "You have no idea how they all esteem this man Carter."

"If he's so good, you should have blown up the damned apartment with everyone in it, then set it alight with gallons of gasoline," the ambassador complained. "You don't kill off a man like that with a frail woman and a knife."

Tsarev rose ponderously. "I'm going to bed. All this talk doesn't do one damned thing for us."

"You will go to bed when I say and not one minute earlier!" Lubkov shouted at him, slamming the window closed.

"Calm down, comrade. What can you do to me?" Tsarev said with a sneer. "Tell them back home that I was insubordinate? Humor the dead man, *tovarich*. Is it too much to ask?"

"Get the hell out of here, both of you," Lubkov said wearily, waving them away. "I'll try to minimize this with the Director, but you'd better come up with something soon."

Nancy Bell opened her eyes to look up at the men standing around her. "You're holding me illegally. I want my lawyer," she said.

Carter was wheeled to the side of her bed by an orderly. His abdomen was supported by a girdle that held his injured internal organs immobile. "Not in this game, sweetheart," he said. "When you play by our rules, you live by our rules."

"God, that makes me sick," she said. "You all treat this like a kind of game for grown men, but you all act like boys."

"Who do you work for?" Hawk asked.

"Stuff it, old man," she snarled at him. This was not the charmer that Carter had escorted the night before. Her lips curled back in scorn. Her bright eyes were dulled by painkillers.

"We can do it the hard way," Carter said. "You just might not survive it."

"What the hell does it matter? You don't fail and go home a hero in my department."

"The 'wet work' didn't quite come off last night," Schmidt commented.

She laughed harshly. "Carter was damned lucky. He moved at just the wrong time," she said. "The bastard should be dead."

"Like all the others who didn't move at just the wrong time," Hawk said. "Come on, Doctor, let's get on with this."

The doctor took a syringe from a sterile towel, depressed the plunger to make sure it was free of air, and pushed it into the intravenous tube already in her arm.

"This isn't admissible," she screamed at them. "Nothing I say under the drug can be used against me."

Carter moved his chair close to her ear. "You've never really played the game, Nancy. We don't have to use this in a court. You're the one who's been playing little girl games. This is for real. We get what we want, then you're nothing but a piece of meat to us."

The others stood silent. They'd never heard Carter

spout such venom. And he was right. But for luck he'd
be dead. And when they had what they wanted, she really
was expendable. Or was she? This one was complicated.

"What's your name?" Schmidt asked when her eyes
closed.

"Nancy Bell."

"And who gave you that name?" Schmidt asked. It
was a routine question with him. They'd been surprised
many times to have a subject come right back with a
second name. Schmidt was going to conduct this one.
He was most familiar with his new drug. "What's your
real name?"

"Sarah Hind," the voice came back uncertainly, almost the voice of a child.

"And how old are you, Sarah?" Schmidt asked.

"I'm ten and a half," the answer came back. "And
I live at One-oh-four Sixth Street."

"Where is that, Sarah?"

"Here. It's right here."

"Do you know the name of the city where you live,
Sarah?" Schmidt asked softly.

"Saddle. I think it's a place called Saddle."

The men looked at each other and shrugged.

"Did your mommy and daddy take you anywhere for
a holiday, a vacation?" Schmidt probed.

"We went to Mount Reindeer once."

Carter leaned over to Schmidt. "Could be Mount Ran-
ier. Not too far from Seattle."

Hawk's face lit up like a light bulb. "Get someone to
check out missing children in Seattle. Use the Sarah Hind
name but be discreet. Just the chief of police—for his
ears only," he whispered to Rupert Smith.

Smith left the room while Schmidt continued. "Why
did you leave Saddle, Sarah?"

The woman's face went blank as if Schmidt had called on a missing part of her life.

"Who is your control?" Carter asked in Russian.

"Yuri Tsarev is my control," she replied immediately in the same language.

"Head of the KGB in Washington," Hawk muttered. "Dear God. What the hell have we got here?"

"Nancy. How many men have you killed?" Schmidt asked.

"I don't know. Haven't counted."

"What about in Washington?" Schmidt asked.

"Have to think about it . . . they move me around. Senator Kantor. Cardinal Yost. Congressman Kilty."

"Ask her about Justice Malone," Hawk whispered to Schmidt.

"But she was a woman," Schmidt responded.

Hawk motioned impatiently.

"Did you kill Justice Malone?"

"Yes."

"Why?"

"They don't give me reasons."

"Why do you think?"

"Stir up unrest between the pro-life and the pro-choice factions. Malone was for abortion. Her vote would have been critical."

"Does Tsarev give you these assignments himself?" Schmidt asked.

"Most of the time. Sometimes I'm sent out from Moscow."

Rupert Smith returned and had a whispered conference with the others. "Confirmed. Sarah Hind disappeared fron Seattle in late 1976. The address checks out. The chief of police wants to know what this is all about."

"So do we. We'll get back to him when we know,"

Hawk said, then turned to Schmidt. "I want you to ask her about her training: where, with whom, for how long—that kind of thing."

"Nancy. You mentioned Moscow. Where did you get your training?"

She screwed up her forehead in thought. "I went to language school first. But we spoke in English all afternoon and at night."

"Where, exactly?"

"First with other kids in Moscow at a big building. Dormitories for girls and boys. It was part of Lumumba."

"Lumumba?" Schmidt asked, surprised. "I thought that was mostly for terrorists."

"It is. This was a new part of Lumumba in Moscow. They have a special *Spetsnaya Naznacheniya* camp at the original Lumumba school now. That was at Pestovo. We trained with army women there."

"Spetsnaz." Carter spit out the word like a curse. "Were the army women Spetsnaz?"

Schmidt maintained exclusive control of her. He repeated the question.

"They were older women. The first women Spetsnaz. They were good."

"How old were you then, Nancy?"

"I was fourteen. They wouldn't take you at the Spetsnaya Naznacheniya until you were fourteen. You had to be able to lift weights, too. I pressed a hundred kilos."

"At fourteen?"

"I had to live in the dormitory until they said I was ready."

"Do you remember your mommy and daddy, Sarah?"

The woman seemed to be struggling with the question in her mind. She didn't answer.

"They probably kept her at the dormitory place until

she'd been brainwashed enough to move on," the doctor suggested. "I'm surprised she remembers her original name and the city of Seattle."

"And she stayed there until she'd learned Russian and was strong enough for battle training," Carter added. "Ask her if she ever killed a political prisoner."

"Why?" Schmidt asked.

"Because the Spetsnaz use humans for bayonet practice—a lot more realistic than using a straw dummy."

"Dear God!" Schmidt said, but he asked the question.

"Yes," she said without emotion. "But not right away. We had to practice a long time before they let us have a prisoner. You had to be able to catch him. They didn't tie him up or anything."

"I don't think we'd better take this much further this time," Schmidt suggested. "I'm not as sure of this drug as I'd like to be."

"One last question, maybe two," Carter suggested. "Ask her if they have a special place for people like her to train before they are finished."

Schmidt asked. The answer was a shocker.

"A long way from Moscow. A long way," she said.

"Was it cold there?" Schmidt asked. "Or was it near the sea?"

"It was cold and it was near the sea."

"I don't understand."

"It was cold outside. But we were inside. We had a whole city under the snow. It was built like a big building, all offices, apartments, and workrooms. We trained there."

"Do you remember a name? Did they ever show you a map?"

"I saw a map once. They built the place so we could

slip into Alaska easily. Chukchi. I think it was called Chukchi.''

Carter motioned them from the bed to a corner of the room. ''I've been there. Even further from Moscow than the gulags of Siberia. Not far from the Bering Strait.''

''The big peninsula across from Alaska?'' Smith asked.

''That's it. But it's one hell of a big place. I suggest we have a concentrated effort by our satellite surveillance teams aimed at that whole area. We need pictures of the place down to the smallest detail. And we need people to go over the pictures.''

Hawk led the way to the lounge where he'd sat with his people the day before. He looked sad, as if he had the cares of the world on his shoulders.

''Are we on the same wavelength?'' Carter asked him.

Hawk looked as if he'd aged ten years in the past hour. ''I don't want to say until I've talked to a few other people. But I think we've got a real stinker here.''

''If the satellites find anything, I'll go in and have a look,'' Carter offered.

''We need a lot of intelligence before then. I want this confirmed from another candidate.''

''Another? Where are you going to get another like her?''

Rupert Smith and Howard Schmidt drank their coffee and stayed out of the conversation for the time being.

''I want in on this. What can I do?'' Carter insisted.

''The doctor says two weeks for you here. And there's no way we'd be ready in less than two weeks anyway.''

''But I'll go stir-crazy in this place.''

''I'm going to get Smitty to talk to the spy satellite people. With the priority we should get, you should have some shots in a couple of days.''

"I'm going to sit here and look at photographs?" Carter asked disgustedly.

"That's the best I can do. Howard will set you up with tables and scanners."

"And what are you going to do?" Carter asked.

Hawk looked at him at first as if he had no intention of telling his plans, but he shrugged and sat across from Carter, his tired eyes looking into the younger man's. "I'll see the President tonight. Either tonight or tomorrow morning early, I'll have a meeting with Fred Lynch and Joe Cronyn."

"Why the deputy directors of the agencies?" Carter said. "Why not go to the top?"

"I can trust these two to work together. You know departmental jealousies, Nick. Both the CIA and FBI have a stake in this. They can both help. I want quick results. I don't want backbiting slowing down this one. Maybe the President can find a way to get the DCI and the FBI director out of the country at the same time."

# THREE

Hawk and Rupert Smith drove out to Langley in Smith's car. They were on the admissions list and admitted by the guard at the gate just before eight in the morning. Hawk called Fred Lynch, the deputy director of operations, right after his late-night meet with the President. Fred called Joe Cronyn and they agreed to meet at Lynch's office at eight.

After parking the car and walking through the ooze of brown slush of the parking lot, the top men from AXE were checked out by a second security station when they entered the lobby. A clean-cut young agent accompanied them up the private bank of elevators that served the DCI, the DDIs, and the DDO. The director of the Central Intelligence Agency and two of his deputy directors were on the seventh floor with the chief of security and all their immediate support staff. The deputy director of operations was on the sixth floor with his department heads and personal staff.

Fred Lynch, the DDO, came out from behind his desk

to greet them. He was about five feet eight, roughly Hawk's height, but about ten years his junior. Lynch and Hawk had been friends for a long time. The DDO always looked serious, though his dry wit was well known to his friends.

"How're you doing?" he asked, holding out his hand to Hawk, then to Smith.

"About the same," Hawk replied. "We always have more then we can handle."

Lynch permitted himself one of his rare smiles. He liked Hawk, and was one of the few at the Company who realized the value of a clandestine outfit that could handle cases too hot for the CIA.

"Know what you mean. We're—" But he was interrupted by the entrance of Joe Cronyn, a big, blustering kind of man whose personality was felt as soon as he entered a room. He was one of the new breed, as far from the Hoover philosophy as possible. He was open and cooperative and one of the best man the FBI had ever had.

They sat around a glass table on a grouping of comfortable chairs. A secretary brought in a tray with a large carafe of coffee and a few mugs. She came and went without a word.

"You didn't give us much to go on, David," Lynch said. "Suppose you lay it all out now."

"Smitty will cover the ground for us," Hawk said. "Then I'd like to map out where we take it from there."

"One of our agents was stabbed." Smith went on to describe the events and the interrogation with just enough detail to cover the subject. Brevity was one of his best qualities.

"So you're convinced this has been a wholesale kidnapping?" Lynch asked.

"The woman described a whole plan, all the way from initial brainwashing to a special facility set up not far from Alaska. They don't set up an underground city as a kind of finishing school unless they have one hell of a lot of people to train," Smith concluded.

"So you're suggesting the Soviets have taken advantage of our runaways to set up a whole new network of spies who were our people originally," Cronyn said. It wasn't put as a question. They had all reached the same conclusion.

"We want some kind of confirmation—at least one more candidate like the woman. Preferably more," Hawk said.

Fred Lynch had been looking thoughtful for the last few minutes. "This has to be kept at our level for the time being, but I may have something. The DCI met with his naval intelligence people yesterday. They caught a kid about nineteen trying to steal top-secret drawings on our new nuclear cruiser," he said. "Been in the service a year and a half, bright, the best kind you could possibly hope to recruit."

"Where do they have him?" Hawk asked.

"The DCI took him off their hands. We've got him downstairs."

"This was yesterday?" Hawk asked. "Maybe we know the kind of questions to ask him now."

They looked at each other and a silent agreement was reached. Lynch led them to the private elevators and pressed the button that would take them to a subbasement. He walked at a steady pace through a maze of corridors and entered a door that required his personal identification pass.

Inside, a guard sat in front of another door. He examined Lynch's identification and asked the others for a palm print. They were all on file and checked out. He pressed an unseen button and allowed them entrance to the inner sanctum.

A place of detention always has a smell of its own. Hawk had never been to the facility, but knew immediately that several prisoners were detained here.

"I want to see the head of your section," Lynch told the guard at the inner door. "These men have the highest clearance."

Even with the DDO's authority, they had to wait several minutes for a man in a white lab coat to appear and greet them. "I was busy with a patient," he said. "What can I do for you?"

Lynch introduced the others and gave the man a brief rundown of their suspicions. Dr. Kevin Wilde was the equivalent of the colonel-doctor who ran the Serbsky Institute in the Soviet Union, the place where all new Soviet truth drugs and interrogation methods were developed and tested.

"We've only done some preliminary work on the boy. You know I like to work up to the problem slowly. We saw no urgency in this one."

"You can see the urgency now. We want him under full interrogation immediately. We'll watch from your observation room."

The place wasn't too different from a hospital setup. The young man was on a gurney. The observers, usually intelligence trainees, were seated behind one-way glass with a full view of the proceedings. A microphone in the room broadcast to the observers.

The young sailor was in blue prisoner garb. He was shackled but made no effort to resist as the shackles were removed and he was transferred to a table similar to those used for operations. It was only a matter of two or three minutes before Dr. Wilde had administered an injection and the boy was in his control.

"Tell me your name, son."

"Leading Seaman Branch Scott, sir."

"No need for naval discipline, son. I'm just your doctor and I need the answers to a few questions."

He let the boy settle down before he proceeded slowly. "Where were you born, Branch?"

"Tacoma."

"That's in the state of Washington."

"Yes, sir."

"All right. When did you leave there, Branch?"

"Came down to enlist when I was eighteen."

"You lived there all your life?"

"I don't know, sir. I had foster parents for a long time."

"In Tacoma?"

"Yes."

"And their name was Scott?"

"Yes."

"Their names, Branch. What were their names?"

"Thelma was my mom. Dad's name was Josh."

Joe Cronyn picked up a phone, reached his office, and relayed the names. He asked for a full-scale rundown on the Scotts that day.

"But you weren't with them long, were you."

The young man seemed to hesitate under the drug. They could see his eyelids flutter and his forehead pucker. "No," he finally said.

"How long did they train you at Lumumba, Branch?"

The question was dropped like a small bomb and it brought a violent reaction. The boy had been passive enough under ankle and wrist restraints, but bucked violently at the question.

"Was Lumumba tough?" Wilde pushed on.

"I *hated* the dormitories. Too many kids. I loved rock, you know? They didn't allow any music."

"But you learned how to make bombs and to kill."

"Yeah, bombs. But not to kill. Learned how to infiltrate, change appearances, contact your control."

"They teach you to speak Russian?"

"They tried. I wasn't good at it. So they put me with English-speaking teachers and trained me faster."

Hawk leaned over to Lynch. "Can we communicate with the doctor?"

"Sure. That microphone," he said, pointing to one side.

"Ask him if they divided them up into those who would be put through fast and those who would be trained slower," he suggested.

The doctor hesitated before the next series of questions.

"Bring in the Spetsnaz," Hawk added.

"Branch. If you could learn Russian, would they keep you longer and train you slower?"

"That's right. I wasn't any good with languages so they called me a low-grade product and I was pulled out of Lumumba."

"And they sent you to the Spetsnaz camp?"

"How did you . . ." Scott seemed more restless than ever. "I didn't like. . . . The old men were turned loose and we had to . . ."

"You had to catch them and kill them."

The young seaman was silent for a long time. "It wasn't my thing. But something about the training, you know? I felt I had to do it."

"How old were you when they took you, son?" the

doctor asked. His mouth was close to the boy's ear, his tone sympathetic.

"I don't remember. We tried to make up calendars but they took them away from us. I think I was about ten."

"So you were in the Soviet Union about seven or eight years."

"Is that where it was? No. I was finished a year before I went to the Scotts. They had me for about fourteen months. They made all the contacts to get me in the navy."

Cronyn picked up the phone again and reached his office. "About my earlier order. Pick up the Scott family, Thelma and Josh, and have them flown to the Hoover Building right away."

He listened for a few seconds.

"Charge then with treason. That should soften them up on the ride down here."

"All right, Branch," the doctor went on. "We're almost finished. Tell me about the underground city where you stayed before they brought you back."

Again, the boy tried feebly to resist the drug but he was no match for the mind-control substance. "It was big. Hundreds of kids. No. Not all kids. Some were real old, like maybe twenty-five."

"How long were you there?"

"How long? I didn't know much about time. It was underground. We slept and we ate and we trained. One cycle after another. If every cycle was a day, maybe I was there a year."

"Did you like it?"

"It was better than Lumumba and that other place where we had to kill old men." He was silent for a long time. The men in the observation room shuffled their feet and fidgeted in their chairs. The doctor was calm as he waited. "We talked a lot, you know? The place was like home, like Tacoma. We talked about about what we could do for 'the cause.'"

"And what was 'the cause,' Branch?"

"To help stop imperialist aggression."

"And what is 'imperialist aggression,' Branch?"

"They—the ones I'm part of now—they are trying to make the world a better place to live. Things like the new cruiser—it will kill a lot of innocent people. We have to stop that."

"So all the people at the underground city have to stop imperialist aggression. They all came with you to do that?"

"Some came with me. Others stayed for more training."

"And how did they bring you out, Branch?"

"It was a cold place. When we came out of the city we were given parkas and arctic boots and stuff. We got on a boat and sailed through the ice for a long time, breaking it, you know? We stopped at night and they took us ashore in small boats. It wasn't as cold then."

"And you went to the Scotts."

"Yes."

"Did they give you the name Scott at the dormitory?"

"Yes. At the dormitory."

The doctor waited a long time before going on. Hawk didn't know the reason for the delay, whether it was emotion or strategy on the doctor's part. He folded his hands on his chest and waited.

"What was your name before the dormitory, Branch?" he finally asked.

"They wouldn't let us say the name ever again. I used to remember, just to fool them. But it slipped away."

Dr. Wilde turned toward the glass and took a few steps away from the patient. "This is apparently a low-grade student assigned the simplest of tasks. I'm surprised they didn't have a rejection program. Maybe they did, but this one slipped through. I'd say he was marginally retarded. Easy for me to spot at this stage, probably not easy for them to spot. They wanted robots and he probably performed to perfection. He looked good to our people for routine tasks, but his low IQ was his downfall here. He wasn't smart enough to be a spy."

Back in Lynch's office they were all silent for a few minutes, each with his own thoughts. Hawk finally broke the silence. "It's diabolical."

"And the worst kind of thing to break up. It's like a cancer," Lynch said. "Even if you could clean out the city, the final staging area, how do you cut off the supply and the ones in the pipeline?"

"We all have to have a part of this," Hawk said. "That much is obvious. My best agent uncovered this. He was chosen as an assassination target by one of their best graduates. They were too confident and they've been tripped up."

"So they'll be pulling in their horns," Smith offered.

"Possibly. But there's lots we can do at the Bureau," Cronyn said. "I'm bringing in the Scott family and we'll find out how the kidnapping conduit and the foster home network operates. I've got a half-dozen families in the Pacific Northwest area under surveillance as possible Soviet plants. They each have at least one teen-ager or young adult."

"Pull them all in right away," Hawk suggested.

"This'll stink to high heaven," Cronyn cautioned.

"Only two groups can make it stink. The media and the Soviets," Smith offered. "First, we keep this from the press, and second, the Soviets can't protest the arrest of American families.''

"We've got to have an overall plan," Hawk observed. "When we've got what we can from the families, my man goes in to nose around. He gathers information on what we can do at each stage of the operation and he either takes action after checking with us, or we come up with a joint plan."

"And why your man?" Lynch asked. "This is CIA business."

"The President doesn't want the CIA identified with this. He told me last night. You can confirm it with him."

Lynch, despite the long-standing friendship, chafed in the role assigned him. His boss, the DCI, would be unhappy about it, but they knew how the President's mind worked. "What else can we do?" he asked.

"Two things. We have to blanket the Chukchi area with satellite flyovers in the next few days. We need treetop resolution. The man I'll be sending in will be examining them for the next couple of weeks, along with your experts, of course. Second, the DCI might have to use his military intelligence groups for the final showdown, and probably military strategists. If and when we locate this place, we have to come up with foolproof solutions to evacuate all our people."

"Unwilling subjects. Fanatics. Killers," Cronyn reminded him.

"But they're *our* people, Joe. Every one of them was an American kid they took from us. Every one has at least one parent who's gone through hell for years."

"God!" Lynch said, as if to himself. "Even if this works, can you imagine the rehabilitation?"

"Imagine instead the alternatives, Fred," Hawk said, biting the end off a cigar and rolling it around in his mouth. "Can you just imagine the result in a few years if we hadn't learned of this?"

"Wait a minute!" Cronyn said. "This finally explains that Alaska thing last June. Remember, Fred?"

"Remember what?" Hawk asked.

They were both silent for a moment or two, then Fred Lynch shook his head as if coming out of a trance and began his recital. "It was one hell of a storm in the Bering Sea. Twenty bodies washed up at a fishing village, all teen-agers. Their fingerprints were all on file with the Registry of Lost Children. All of their clothes had been bought at the same store in Seattle. They were traced to families in the Pacific Northwest." He paused for a moment, taking off his glasses and rubbing his eyes. "We were baffled at the time. Why would they show up together? Why the clothes from the same store?"

"And now we know," Cronyn finished for him. "They were being transported to foster homes after their training. Their boat must have been sunk in the storm."

"But why no seamen?" Hawk asked. "They couldn't have come in by themselves."

"No foreign seamen were reported among the missing. Ten men died in that area as well as others along the whole western shore."

"That's bad news," Smith said, rubbing his chin with his right hand.

"What are you thinking, Smitty?" Hawk asked.

"If no Soviet seamen were found, then the men transporting the kids were local seamen."

# FOUR

Huge envelopes filled with satellite photos started to show up every day at the Virginia facility. They arrived by special CIA armored courier. Carter had been given permission to walk the grounds the second day, and from the third day every time he needed a break from the drudgery of paper work he managed a short dogtrot around the hospital building. The air was crisp; the thin ground cover of snow was no problem.

He had two long tables to work on and a twelve-inch-square illuminated magnifying glass. Scanning photos hour after hour seemed an endless and tedious task, and he didn't envy agents he'd known who'd spent most of their lives doing it, all the way back to the days of U2 flyovers.

What he saw in one picture after the other was snow and more snow. Tracks led him from village to village where he could see the locals enduring what must have been subzero temperatures to perform any task outdoors. He didn't see many people outside and the number of vehicles in the barren countryside was limited. This was the equivalent, probably worse, of life on the shores of the Arctic Ocean in northern Alaska or Canada's Northwest Territories in winter. Scratch that. Even the lowliest Eskimo or Inuit had a snowmobile. To find a snowmobile track in the backwoods of Chukchi was an event.

On the fifth day he was feeling much better physically. It was confirmed that the liver was healing rapidly and his two-week stay could be shortened. The boredom was also broken by a visit from Howard Schmidt.

The big man who spent most of his time in his basement domain in the Dupont Circle headquarters of AXE was a man Carter liked and admired. At those times when Schmidt insisted AXE's crack agent spend hours boning up on new information about the enemy—agents recently identified, weapons recently introduced—he could gladly do without him, although the information had invariably proved useful. Most of the time Schmidt's gadgets had saved his neck, and while Carter kidded the big man about his wild imagination, he'd be hard pressed to operate without the weird contraptions Schmidt devised to give AXE agents the edge.

"What's going on outside these walls?" Carter asked. "I'm going nuts in here."

"The FBI have raided a half-dozen houses in the Pacific Nortwest and have the occupants in custody. I don't know what they've learned in detail, but Hawk briefed us last night and we know we're on the right track."

Carter led Schmidt away from the piles of photos to a place where they could smoke. He lit a cigarette and sat back, relaxed. Schmidt took out an old pipe and held it in his hand, rubbing the cherrywood, coming as close as he ever did to lighting it.

An orderly who'd taken a particular liking to Carter

came in with two mugs of coffee. "You want cream or sugar?" he asked.

They both shook their heads and the young man left.

"I've been thinking about the next few steps," Schmidt started. He drew the pipe against the side of his nose and rubbed the natural body oil into the shining red wood with a thumb.

"Me too. It's not often I get this much time to think," Carter said, leaning into the soft chair, easing his cramped back. "Usually Ginger calls, or Hawk, and I'm off somewhere within hours."

"We've got to know so much on this one. What does the Lumumba school look like? How does it operate? Do they have special barracks and special instructors at the Spetsnaz camp? And where the hell is it? Why would they build an underground city close to Alaska as the final training ground for the kids when they could have built it anywhere and just transported them to a staging area close to our shores?"

Carter dragged on his cigarette and tossed the questions around in his head. He'd been thinking along the same lines and had taken it a step further. "I'll need some high-powered credentials to gain access to Lumumba. That means authentic Soviet clothes for a special inspector of the KGB. Do you remember scheduling me to read up on the whole KGB organization again last year?"

"Not specifically."

"Let me quote from your own files. This is from the responsibilities of the First Chief Directorate: *The Ninth Department concentrates on surveillance and recruitment of foreign students. To this end, it enlists informants among the faculties and student bodies of all Soviet universities. On occasion, Soviet students have bravely con-*

*fided to Americans that they were informants and explicitly warned them about KGB traps.''*

Schmidt was aware of Carter's photographic memory but was seldom witness to the result. He was impressed, but it was in keeping with the aura surrounding the man who had almost become a myth within the agency. "So what do you conclude?" he asked.

"That this operation, whatever it is, has probably sprung from some new leadership in the Ninth Department. It's probably related to Gorbachev's shakeup of the KGB last year. I'd like our people in Moscow to give us all they can on the Ninth Department, including pictures of its chief personnel. Most important, are any of them out of the country right now? Do any of them travel constantly? Maybe one of them is in charge of this new operation."

"And you're going to impersonate him."

"Looks like a good bet. If I had enough pictures of the man, I could become him, even gain access to vital information on the strengths and locations of the schools they employ."

"So my part is clothing and makeup."

"I'll need a liaison who can supply me with weapons and explosives anywhere in the USSR."

"That's one hell of a tough order."

"But you can do it, Howard. Use that fertile mind of yours and come up with some tricks of your trade that will help me."

Schmidt held the pipe with both hands, his elbows on the table, his coffee mug empty. He loved a challenge and this one was shaping up as one of the best. "Give me some scenarios," he said, an inscrutable expression on his face.

"One: They have a network to pick up kids at this end

and transport them to Mother Russia. I'd have guessed
that they'd have screened them first, but the kid they
picked up in the navy didn't seem too bright. Two: They
have an initial indoctrination area where they brainwash
the kids and start the process of evaluating them, even
to the point of disposing of some. Three: After indoctrination they proceed to the Lumumba annex, or whatever it is, to start their education. This would be the first
hands-on use of weapons and exposure to violence for
most of these kids. Four: They are shipped off to the
Spetsnaz school. By this time they are hardened to violence and death. The special forces of the Soviet army
must have trained specialists to train kids. Last: They
end up in the underground city to refresh them on American life. I suspect they also receive specialist training
here. Nancy Bell was probably trained as a hit person
because she had the looks and the aptitude.

"Let me tell you, old buddy, I was damned lucky to
survive her knife. She had me completely fooled. Imagine what she'd be like when she went up against a civilian."

"What are we going to do with her?" Schmidt asked.

"What are we going to do with all of them? That's
the toughest problem. They'll probably send me in there
to wipe out the organization, but how do I save the kids?
How do I save kids who have been trained to hate Americans and kill in a thousand ways?"

"I expect the FBI will take care of the kidnapping ring
at this end. I don't know what you're going to do about
the kids they already have in their hands."

"I've been thinking about Delta Force. The antiterrorist group is sitting at Fort Bragg or Smoky Mountain
in a constant state of readiness, just itching for something
like this," Carter mused aloud as he lit another cigarette.

"What do you have in mind?"

"I don't know—not yet. I can see them coming into the Chukchi area in force and taking the whole school of kids back. I can't see them in the heart of Moscow, so that's out. For them to be used aginst the best troops in the Soviet Union, it'll depend on where the Spetsnaz camp is located. They couldn't fly thousands of miles over the USSR either in or out."

"You're assuming a lot, Nick. All this is based on some drug-induced confessions from the girl and the kid in the navy, right?"

"Yeah, but that's all we've got to go on. I'm going to let the doctor have one more crack at the girl. She'll know the name of the Soviet officer in charge over there. We've got to take every opportunity we can get," Carter said, getting up to stretch. "It might all be supposition, but I'd bet a month's pay that most of my assumptions are right."

"So I'll get back to my dungeon and start preparing your equipment."

The phone rang on one of the desks. While Carter had been meticulous about keeping all the photos in sequence, the phone had become a victim of the volume of prints. He found it on the fifth ring.

"Carter."

"This is Charlie at recon. We've found it."

"Great! Is it in the batch I got this morning?"

"Yes. Check out shots NW/SE 141 to 145. Call me when you've had a chance to look them over."

"Good work, Charlie. I'll get back to you."

"They've found the underground city," Schmidt said.

"Right. And it means that the woman's information is valid. I'm going to look over the photos and set up another interrogation."

"Let me know what you find. I'll be working on my end."

When Schmidt had gone, Carter sifted through the hundreds of photos and found shots NW/SE 141 to 145. He piled all the others at the end of one table and concentrated on the five glossies spread out before him.

The photos had a scale at the top right-hand corner set in place by the camera based on its altitude. Carter used a ruler and measured the size of the circle that was most evident on the photo labeled 143. He could tell the size of the dome, or whatever it was, because it was totally clear of tracks. Trucks had moved to and from two directions to the circle that was about a half mile across. He examined the other four shots but couldn't tell if the tracks came from a specific direction or if they converged at some point.

He picked up the telephone and punched in seven numbers.

"Charlie."

"I've looked at it, Charlie. Good piece of work. Now, has anyone looked at all the photos within ten miles and learned if the two sets of tracks converge?"

"We'd thought of it."

"When you find it, find out the closest village and send me a set of topographical maps that shows its location on the peninsula."

"Can do. We'll be taking fresh shots of the area every time our satellite makes a pass. It's been kept on an orbit that will give us new shots every ninety minutes."

"Don't send them all to me. Just the maps and photos that show any significant change."

"Will do."

"One more thing. Can you try for more resolution now?"

"Sure. What do you want?"

Carter thought about it for a minute. "I've heard that you get the best results in cold weather, so I'm expecting some real closeups. I know you can't give me faces, but I'd like to see the rank of the military personnel who come and go. Do any of the vehicles fly pennants? Can we read the markings on the trucks? Do they have an airstrip nearby? How far away is it and how long are the runways? Anything at all that will help."

"No problem, buddy. This can be one boring job, you know? When we get one like this, we all go a little nuts. You'll be fighting us off before you're finished."

"Thanks." He put down the receiver. That part of his job was done. He'd have to talk to Hawk later in the day and set up a time for the doctor to help him with Nancy Bell. Maybe he'd even have some quiet chats with her before they used the drug again. The experience might be enlightening.

It was going well. Now, if they'd let him out of here soon, maybe he could start the first part of the assignment. He was eager to get going.


Nancy Bell was sitting in a chair beside her bed, a whiplash collar around her neck, her right arm in a sling.

"I wondered how long it would take you to come," she said, her expression giving no clues as to her feelings.

"I've been busy."

"You don't look too bad for an invalid."

"I was lucky. I searched your whole apartment for a weapon. The flesh-colored knife was very clever."

"They told me you were the best. I thought you were totally absorbed. How did you know?"

He wasn't about to admit to sheer luck. It wasn't a matter of pride. You just never gave the enemy any ammunition, even when it appeared they'd be in custody forever. "I'm trained to be suspicious," he said. "I kept on the move. Another few seconds and I'd have found the knife myself," he lied. It wasn't a total lie. His hands *had* been busy.

"And I'd have acted sooner, but I have to admit . . ."

"We both have to admit . . ." he said, smiling for the first time.

She was blushing. He was surprised. "You killed some of our top people," he said, his expression and feelings back to normal.

"And you've killed some of our best. That's why they sent me after you."

"But that's different. You were born here. They changed you into a tool."

"So they told me here. And I've spent long hours sitting here thinking about it. I don't feel I've done anything wrong. I don't know exactly what they did, but I'm not the kid Sarah Hind they say I am. I'm Nancy Bell, associate librarian at the Library of Congress, special agent of the KGB, trained just as you are, sent out just as you are."

"So what do you think we should do with you?"

"I honest-to-God don't know. Listen, put yourself in my place. Forget about the kidnapping crap. If you were sitting here you'd be planning your escape, right? How can you expect me to be any different?"

"You tell me. I need to know a great deal about the setup over there. What's the name of the man in the Ninth Department who runs the show? How old is he? What does he look like? Does he do a lot of traveling?"

Her eyes flashed momentarily when he mentioned the Ninth Department, so he knew he scored one point, but the rest was useless. "Go to hell, Carter. You don't get

it, do you? I'm really one of them. I'm going to get the
hell out of here and I'm going to kill you.''

Three hours later, Nancy Bell was stretched out on
the same gurney they'd used for the first interrogation.
Dr. Cathy Simms was substituting for the doctor who'd
been there the first day. She'd been Carter's attending
physician almost from the first day. She'd examined the
wounds and the bandages daily and was the one who'd
decided he could move about sooner than he'd expected.

The needle slid into the intravenous tubing that had
been prepared earlier. The questions that Carter wanted
answered had been discussed in advance. When Nancy
was under, and she'd gone without a fuss, Dr. Simms
nodded at him.

"I'm in Moscow, Nancy. I'm standing in front of
Lubyanka Prison and the old KGB headquarters at Two
Dzerzhinsky Square. I'm walking toward the Serbsky
Institute of Forensic Psychiatry and standing back, look-
ing at the imposing steel fence and gates that guard it.
Our old friend Colonel-Doctor Luntz is still well and
business goes on there as usual. Did you ever see inside
Serbsky, Nancy?''

She shuddered from the horror the name conjured up.
The reply was a weak "No."

"I have. Not a very nice place. Did your colonel come
from Serbsky?''

"He's worked there.''

"Under Luntz?''

"I don't know.''

"What is his name, Nancy.''

"We're not supposed to know.''

"You can tell me, Nancy. You can trust me.''

Carter sat back in a comfortable chair that he had

placed so he could be close to her ear. Proximity made the interview more real, more comfortable, and helped the subject identify with the concern, real or imagined, of the interrogator.

"I saw him once. Colonel Simolin."

"Did you ever hear his full name?"

"Yes."

"Repeat it, please."

"Colonel-Doctor Nikolai Leonid Simolin."

"Thank you, Nancy. What did he look like?"

"I was afraid of him."

"You were trained to remember details. Tell me about his size, his features."

The answer came slowly. "With his hat on he looked tall, more than six feet three. The hat would add about two or three inches. He was not fat, but he had on a greatcoat, so I couldn't tell. His face was not Slavic—more like my foster father's."

"The one called Bell?"

"Just like him. They were like twins."

Carter was pleased with that little gem. "What about the man who ran the last place you were at—the underground city?"

"Everyone hated Colonel Sobolev. He was a brute."

"What did he look like?"

She thought for a long moment. "I've seen a Rambo movie since I came here. He was like Rambo with very short hair. His mouth curled in the same way when he talked. His body was muscular, though he was three or four inches taller."

"Did you see their eyes?"

"Colonel Sobolev's eyes were brown. I'll never forget those eyes."

"Simolin's eyes. What about them?"

"Blue. Not light or dark—medium blue."

"What was the bad one's full name?"

"They called him 'the bastard.' "

Carter waited, knowing she'd answer eventually.

"Colonel Igor Victor Sobolev. I hated him. I could kill him without hesitation."

Carter motioned to the doctor and they talked in a far corner of the room.

"I'm going to recommend that you nursemaid this one," he said. "When I'm over there I might want to call in for some information she's got buried in that pretty head."

"Can do. Will I get to talk to you?"

"I doubt it. Dictate it into computer memory. Use her name as the password. The computer will repeat your message word-for-word if I give the password."

"Are you finished here?" she asked, glancing at Nancy Bell.

"Finished."

Dr. Cathy Simms threw the spent syringe into the paper lining of a wastebasket and covered Nancy with a light blanket, then called for an orderly to have the prisoner returned to her room.

# FIVE

The photos had arrived several times a day with almost clockwork regularity. The topographicals had been marked up with a red grease pencil. The experts at the CIA shop had calculated that the "dome" was a hill that had been used for a crown to cover an underground city. They had also included studies of the soil content of the area. It was tundra country, frozen solid in winter but soft and filled with moisture in the summer, a layered, shifting surface that could not be used as a foundation. The only solution they could come up with was an excavation carved out of the ground in winter and coated with either cement or some kind of sprayed silicone.

He pored over each new batch of photos, looking for any clue that might help later, but he came up with very little. The vehicles that he saw occasionally were supply trucks. He was able to make a rough estimate of the supplies brought in daily, enough to support a population of about five hundred. But that seemed impossible in such a remote area. The dome was no more than fifty miles from the Chukchi shore. Big Diomede Island and Little Diomede Island were less than a hundred miles away. The two islands, one Soviet and the other American, were less than five miles from each other.

Some of the shots were useless, taken during blizzard conditions, but they invariably showed new tracks and new patterns later, in the fresh snow. Carter affirmed his calculations and decided he had nothing further to gain from the photos.

He rang for the nurse, who showed up in seconds.

"I'm checking myself out. Who's on duty?"

"Dr. Simms. But I don't think . . ."

"Just tell her I'm leaving. Okay?"

The young woman shrugged and left his room. Carter had his clothes on before Dr. Cathy Simms was at his door, scowling at him.

He held up a hand to forestall any lecture. "I'm fine. I've got to get out of here."

She smiled and shook her head. "I know better than to argue with the great Nick Carter. But you're basically in good shape, and you've had a rest. And to show I mean it, I'll sign you out myself."

Carter grabbed his toilet kit and jacket, and kissed her on the forehead. "Thanks, Doc," he said.

Dr. Simms blushed, and smiled coyly up at him. "On the other hand, you are nice to have around . . ." she said with a chuckle.

He grinned and kissed her lightly on the lips, then they walked to the office to complete the paper work that would send him on his way.

Carter drove directly to Dupont Circle, parked three blocks away, and after a careful recon around the neighborhood, called Hawk from the general office downstairs.

"Nick?" Ginger Bateman said. "How are you feeling?"

"Almost normal. I thought I'd check the mood before I came up."

"The old man's in excellent spirits. I think he was about to call you. Let me check."

She was gone for about a minute. "He says meet him around back. His driver will be waiting."

Hawk made it to the car in his express elevator almost as fast as Carter could walk through the crowded general office.

"What's up?" he asked.

"Joe Cronyn has a bunch of people detained. He's got them under wraps on the top floor of the Holiday Inn near the Naval Observatory in Georgetown."

"The ones from around Tacoma and Seattle?"

"The same."

They drove down New Hampshire Avenue to Juarez Circle, across the Rock Creek bridge, and were on Wisconsin Avenue in minutes.

The parking lot was crowded, but the only people in sight seemed disinterested in their surroundings. Appearances to the contrary, they were some of Cronyn's best operatives and alert to every movement. They recognized Hawk, but checked out his identification anyway. They were disturbed that Carter had no identification on him, but they finally let them both in on the strength of Hawk's reputation.

Cronyn met them in the lobby. "We've got the whole top floor and one elevator blocked off."

"I don't like the look of it," Hawk growled. "Desk clerks and bellhops make money from newshounds for information like this. You could have this place crawling with the media at any moment."

"You could be right. One of my senior people took it upon himself to set it up."

"I'd look long and hard at his record, Joe. In the meantime, get them to one of your safe houses."

"I'll do it one at a time after we interview them."

The first three families were practically carbon copies: mother and father middle income, mother at home, father at a store as an assistant manager or at a bank. The kid was usually between sixteen and eighteen, a high school honor student. All model citizens.

The fourth was different. They were in a suite. The father was a stockbroker, the mother a lawyer, and the daughter a senior at the University of Washington.

The father was belligerent, a big man, boisterous, blustering about the people he knew, the connections he had in government. The wife was almost as difficult. She was president of the Washington State Bar Association. Her threats were couched in legalese that had no effect whatsoever on Cronyn, Hawk, or Carter.

"I'd suggest we have Mr. Big Mouth and Madame President taken to another room while we interview their daughter," Hawk said, his voice cold. "They can talk all they want. They can call anyone they want. We've got them cold and they'll serve a long time in separate cells," he said. It was untypical of him, intended as an opening gambit for the girl.

They left meekly. The three men stood looking down on the college student.

"What's your name, young lady?" Cronyn asked, his tone harsh.

"Are you who I think you are?" she asked, avoiding his question.

"I am. And that should show you how important I consider this case."

"Case, Mr. Deputy Director? What case?"

She wasn't looking at Cronyn, she was sizing up Hawk, the one strong enough to cow her domineering parents. Then she turned her devastating green eyes on Carter. She kept her expression in neutral while looking him over. She was a natural redhead with alabaster skin, and was probably about five-feet-six or seven.

Carter imagined the Russians had considered this girl one of their prize pupils, giving her time to experience several years at a local university before she infiltrated the higher echelons of ... what? Would it be government? That was his bet. This one could charm her way to the top. He'd bet she'd be capable of anything.

"I'd like to talk to Miss Hodgson alone," Carter said, not taking his eyes from hers for a moment.

Cronyn started to object, but Hawk knew his man and guided the bigger man out by the elbow.

"How do you like the university, Alice," Carter asked, sitting opposite her and picking one of his custom-blended cigarettes from a gold case.

"May I have one of those?" she asked.

He handed her a cigarette and flamed it for her. She took a long, deep drag and held the cigarette out for a close inspection. "Only one man in the world smokes these—if he's not an imposter, that is."

"You didn't answer my question. I've been there. Beautiful campus. Looks out over Union Bay. Lots of trees. A great place to take a girl sailing on a Sunday afternoon."

"They told us about you. I'm flattered that you'd single me out for interrogation."

"They told you? About my cigarettes? What else?"

"That you were terrific in bed. The best agent in the

business on either side. Nancy Bell's a friend of mine. I hope she's being treated well."

"Rehabilitation," he said. "She's in good hands."

"Poor Nancy. She believed it all, went for it all the way."

"And you didn't?"

"No way. I've been back three years while Nancy's been working at setting you up. I've had three years of the good life, getting used to being back."

"What about the two who just left?"

"Robots. Been in place a long time. Don't understand anything but the doctrine."

"And you do?"

"I never fell for the line."

"And you never went to the Spetsnaz camp? You were never trained there?"

"I had to go through the rituals. If not, I'd have been weeded out and dead."

"Not necessarily," he said in Russian. "They'd have assigned you to a less ambitious program."

"You're sure of that?" she answered in the same language. "If you showed real promise, and I was near the top, you were a dead hunk of meat if you dogged it. So I went along."

"Where was the Spetsnaz camp?" he asked, reverting to English.

"They've designed a camp near Pestovo, about half-way between Moscow and Leningrad."

"But the political prisoners. I thought they'd be at the gulags."

"They don't all get that far, Carter. You're as naïve as the men who were taken out of their beds at night and thrown into Lubyanka. They think the worst that can happen to them is a few years in the gulags. Most of them don't get that far.''

"So the targets weren't prisoners wearied by years of starvation and work?''

"There's no sport in that, Carter. They were fresh from Lubyanka in Moscow. Some were well fed and strong.''

Carter thought about the horror of what she'd described and if it were possible to rehabilitate one like this. ''And you're telling me you never bought the party line?''

"You've got it. They're animals.''

"Christ, Alice! Then why continue the charade here? You could have walked into any FBI office and opened up the whole scheme.''

She took a drag on the half-smoked cigarette and flipped ash on the carpet. ''Do you think they'd believe me? I'd tell them about Lumumba, the Spetsnaz thing, and the Chukchi camp. They'd have put me in a straitjacket.''

"What do they call the Chukchi camp?'' Carter asked.

"They called it Kivak, but we were about fifty miles inland from Kivak. If you've got us, you probably know where it is.''

"Too bad,'' he thought aloud.

"Too bad what, Nick Carter?''

"Too bad you're one of them. You'd be a great help in closing down the whole operation.''

"So? Why can't I?''

"Don't be a fool, Alice. You're too far gone. You'd turn me in as soon as we arrived in Moscow.''

"You still don't get it, do you? I fooled them. I was never really under their control.''

"Bullshit. If I believed that, you'd have made a beeline

for your real parents right away and turned in the Hodg-sons.''

The tears were coming now. He should have suspected it. She was a great actress, probably one of their best students ever.

''That's the one thing they succeeded in. They blocked out my real name somehow. I don't know who my parents were. I've tried and tried, but that part is lost forever.''

''Along with integrity, belief in democracy, all the freedoms. You're a real case, Alice. You called them robots. You're so damned obvious you stink,'' he said, getting up and locking her in the room.

He went back to a lounge where Cronyn and Hawk were waiting. He told them the conversation, almost word-for-word.

''What if there's some truth in her story?'' Cronyn suggested.

''If she's for real, she'd be one hell of an asset,'' Hawk mused.

''You don't believe that for a minute, do you?'' Carter asked.

''Tell you what,'' Hawk said. ''Let's give her to Fred Lynch. Dr. Wilde takes a day or two to turn her inside out. She shapes up, she goes with you.''

Within six hours, they were sitting in two comfortable chairs at the White House opposite the chief executive himself.

''So you see, Mr. President, it's a very complex sit-uation,'' Hawk said, concluding his recital of the details they had.

''It would appear that the children at Lumumba are not as brainwashed as later, but the situation permits no chance for getting them out,'' the President said.

"You can never be sure until you are on the scene," Carter added.

"Give me a quick scenario right off the top of your head," the President said.

Carter took a few seconds to organize his thoughts. "I will have the credentials of a major of the Ninth Department of the First Chief Directorate, or I might hold similar rank in the department of the Inspector General. I use a diversion to get all the children into the Metro a block from the new Lumumba installation. Dozens of embassy cars meet them at the underground station near the embassy and whisk them inside."

"What then?"

"You asked for a scenario, not a solution. I'll devise a plan when I'm on the scene. This time a helper would be welcome."

"I understand the Hodgson girl might be a good candidate," the President suggested.

"She's still an unknown quantity, Mr. President. If she comes through the interrogation, she's a good bet. We're a day or two away from that decision."

The President must have pressed a button, for a secretary appeared as if summoned. "Send Fred Lynch in," he asked.

"Fred," the President started without any preliminaries when the DDO had walked in. Lynch nodded to Hawk and Carter, then took a seat close to the door. "I've been filled in on this horrible business by you, by Joe Cronyn, and now David. What I want to know is this: Do you have anyone on the scene who could help Mr. Carter? Considering the situation—the ages of the youngsters—it might be good to have a woman involved."

Carter fidgeted in his chair. He'd have preferred to

make the decision and the choice. But when the big boss talked, you listened.

"I've got the perfect agent in place. Sue Setzel. She's been there about a month. They don't really know of her yet. Lots of experience. An innovative agent. Speaks about seven languages."

"Sounds too good to be true, Fred," Hawk kidded. "We may just try to recruit her."

"I want to talk some more to David and Mr. Carter," the President said. "But I have a position I want you all to know before you leave, Fred." He sipped his coffee before continuing.

"I don't want any loose ends on this one. I want every American child brought back, whatever the cost. I'm not concerned about Soviet-American relations in this. The hell with diplomatic kid gloves! The bastards have stolen our kids!" He pounded on the antique desk behind which he sat.

"None of us do, Mr. President," Fred Lynch said on his way out. "We'll go all-out on this one."

"I'm interested in this camp you've described, Mr. Carter. You say they could have five hundred young people down there?"

"Five hundred in the installation, sir. We don't know how many are trainees, but the ones who are there— perhaps between one and two hundred—they'll all be close to the end of their training," Carter reminded him.

"So how can we get them out?" the President asked.

"I've got several ideas about that. I can get them to the surface, but what do I do with them when they're all out?"

"Explain," the President said, leaning forward.

"Suppose I get in there posing as a Soviet officer. Maybe I have help and maybe I don't. I set a number of explosive charges or poison gas bombs and then tell them to get out to save their lives," Carter said, hesitating while he took a drink of the coffee that was getting cold. "I've got them all topside in the frozen tundra. Scores, maybe hundreds of guards with AK-47s will be milling around in the snow with nowhere to go."

The President thought about it for a few minutes. The silence in the Oval Office was like the snow that drifted down outside. "You know what I've got, Mr. Carter?" he finally said, his face breaking into a smile. "I've got about five hundred of the best-trained antiterrorist soldiers in the world all sitting on their duffs at Fort Bragg bored out of their gourds."

Carter knew where he was going with this one and had to get his two cents in. "What you're thinking would be an armed invasion of the Soviet Union."

"Like God told Paul when the preacher scored a hole in one early on a Sunday morning, Carter: 'Who's he going to tell?'"

"I like it," Hawk said.

The President picked up the phone and spoke to his secretary. "Get me the Chairman of the Joint Chiefs of Staff on the line and patch us in with the man who commands Delta Force. I believe his name's Colonel Ballard."

# SIX

The next day, Carter and Hawk made the trip to North Carolina in a CIA Gulfstream IV. They were accompanied by one of Fred Lynch's agents with an attaché case chained to his wrist. Carter was more amused than annoyed. The boys in the big agencies had a tendency to be paranoid about security at times.

They landed at Fort Bragg, were met by a GM Suburban with dark glass windows and driven for more than a half hour before Hawk asked the driver, "Where the hell are we going, boy?"

"The colonel's at Smoky Mountain Camp, sir. We use both facilities. He thought you'd have more privacy up there."

Carter sat looking out of the dark glass as they proceeded from a main highway to a rugged gravel road covered with a few inches of packed snow. The Suburban had four-wheel drive and the driver was wisely using power to all four wheels. It also had front and back heaters that were both in operation. "Notice anything about the terrain?" he asked Hawk.

"Snow is not my favorite commodity," the older man replied.

"Plenty of snow and a lot of these knolls could be like the one called Kivak."

"That's their problem, Nick. If it becomes their problem."

The Suburban was stopped at a checkpoint and passed through after identification. They drove on for another three or four minutes, past barracks blocks, parade grounds, mock aircraft, and gutted buildings obviously used for assault training. They stopped at the last building in the compound, close to the high wire fence, its back against an almost vertical rock formation.

Colonel Jamie "Crunch" Ballard came out to meet them. He'd played guard for Army at 260 pounds. Fifteen years later he was down to 220, every ounce vital and functioning perfectly. Even his short wiry hair seemed to stand at attention waiting for action orders. The man exuded strength and power. He was an inch or so shorter than Carter, and was a "no-neck." His shoulders and head seemed to be one, having no need for a bridge between them. His eyes were a bright blue as he took in the three visitors at a glance and held out a hand.

"James Ballard," he said, talking to Hawk first, according the senior man all the courtesy he deserved. They shook hands. "Mr Carter," he said, taking the Kill-master's hand in his in a contest of strength. Carter suspected everything on the base was a test of strength. He allowed the colonel the win, feeling no compunction to waste energy on pecking-order games.

Ballard didn't acknowledge the CIA courier but waved them all to follow him in. He was billeted in large log structure that was something out of ski country, but more Kentucky log lodge than alpine in design. The main room where he took them was filled with comfortable furniture, a mixture of cowhide covering and floral prints. Carter remembered reading that the colonel's wife was on the base with him. A long table was set up against one wall. A monstrous fireplace took up most of another wall. Logs at least four feet in length were crackling in it, giving off a dancing light and making the room smell like a ski lodge.

"Leave the case on the long table," the colonel said, speaking to the courier for the first time. "If you need a signature, see my orderly."

When the man had gone, Ballard offered them a drink. "Can't stand the bloody red tape in the agencies. Imagine sending a courier all the way down here with you. Damn fool bureaucracies."

Carter was amused but kept his feelings to himself. He agreed it had been an unnecessary caution, that they were hidebound by bureaucratic nonsense a lot of the time. But he'd learned long ago not to expend energy fighting city hall. It was a losing game. He also noted the word *bloody* and reminded himself that a lot of the Delta people had received their initial training at Bradbury Lines in England, home of the famed Special Air Services, SAS, the 22nd Regiment, probably the best fighting men in the world before groups like Delta Force had been assembled.

"We live and die by bureaucracies, Colonel. I find you ride with them or you go over the edge," Hawk observed, echoing Carter's thoughts.

"You haven't had to sit on your butts while politicians debate your fate. They've been bloody consistent. They've invariably decided against using our expertise."

"Except once," Hawk reminded him.

"Sure. The desert in Iran." Ballard waved a muscled arm. "A fiasco. And all because we were forced to use a makeshift force. The planes weren't ours. The choppers weren't ours. The whole thing was a patchwork," he said disgustedly. "Never again. When Delta moves, it uses Delta equipment and is under my exclusive command."

"The President had no qualms about using your force when we explained the problem," Hawk told him. "That's why we're here."

"Thank God for change. A new administration, gentlemen. And a new Chairman of the Joint Chiefs of Staff, an army man who's had faith in us for years." He topped up their drinks and led them to the long table, turning on an overhead light. "Let's see what you've brought with you," he said eagerly, taking the chair at the head of the table, his eyes bright with anticipation.

The courier had opened the case with Ballard's orderly and it lay open like a shucked oyster. Carter pulled out the latest set of pictures, alive with marker pencil jottings, and the topographical maps of the area.

"First an overview," Carter said. He felt he had to impart motivation from the beginning. "More than a million American kids are reported missing every year. Most are taken by parents after custody battles. Some teen-agers just run away and roam the streets. But we've learned that the Soviets have exploited our weakness and have been kidnapping our kids for years."

"The bastards," Ballard breathed, his attention riveted on Carter.

"This is our baby, Colonel. But it's so big we've got to cut you a piece of the pie."

"I think my men are going to love this."

Carter skipped over the initial kidnapping, the Lumumba school, and the Spetsnaz involvement to get to the final phase. "It's my job to infiltrate. I'm not set on how to handle the first two phases, but the last one seems clear to me."

"What's that?" Ballard asked, his enthusiasm building.

Carter explained the satellite photos, and gave Ballard his estimates and those of the CIA experts. He moved on to the topographical maps and showed Ballard the location of the airport, the defenses, and the contours of the surrounding countryside.

"What's the plan up to now?" Ballard asked.

"You can't gain entry and kill off all the guards. Not like a hostage rescue. All our own people—they'll be teen-agers or in their twenties—will have received full Soviet indoctrination. If they're armed, they'll be as much of a threat as the guards.

"I've got several scenarios in mind. I can infiltrate with no problem. I can even carry enough plastique inside to blow the place to hell. Or I can fill the place with gas. My preference is to set charges, then warn them all to get the hell out. The timing would have to be perfect. You'd have to be on the ground and ready to subdue them as soon as they hit the surface."

"Why not gas them and let us go in and carry them out?" Ballard suggested.

"I've been involved in things like this before, Colonel. Not anything as big where we had to rescue our own, but big enough. The problem has always been transport. We don't know what we're going to find down there. We force them to walk or run to the surface themselves and your men have a cleanup job to do. If we gas them, you've got to have one man to carry and one to guard.

Besides, it would take a lot longer and we'll be in enemy territory with radar tracking you in.''

Ballard looked at Carter with new respect. "With radar tracking, our C-32s could be shot down before they hit the airport.''

"The CJCS has promised an air umbrella. He's determined to get these kids back.''

"Okay. I've got the outline of the Kivak raid. But what about a crack at the Spetsnaz? Any of my men would give his right arm to show the Spetsnaz who's best.''

"And it could take the right arm of most of them—maybe the lives of some others,'' Carter said. "You've got one hell of a chance to pull off the Kivak job with minimal casualties. But I don't even know yet where the Spetsnaz camp is. With Kivak you'll have full intelligence and air cover. We'll have to talk about your further involvement when I know a lot more.''

"Good enough, Carter. When are you going in?''

"Next few days. We haven't firmed it up yet.''

"How much time do I have?''

"I don't know. But I'd say two weeks at the least.''

"We saw plenty of areas on the way in that are a lot like the target area except for one thing,'' Hawk contributed.

"What's that?''

"Trees. Mostly tundra at Kivak.''

"We've got a part of the camp killed off by a forest fire a year before we moved in. It's not been reforested yet.''

"We're leaving this data with you,'' Hawk said. "You can have updates of the photos flown in as often as you want.''

"Sounds good. Anything else?'' Ballard asked.

"Yes. Practice with gas masks in place part of the time," Carter said. "We might have to saturate the surface with gas. I don't know any other way to keep from killing our own."

"How are the winds in the target area?" Ballard asked.

"Not good. Never a calm day. But our meteorologists will be able to give us good data a day ahead. Mostly the winds are constant, west to east."

"Could help," Ballard conceded.

Hawk stood. "We've got to get back. My desk is loaded with other projects," he said.

"Thanks for the job," Ballard said.

Hawk allowed his features to manufacture one of his rare smiles. It looked out of place on his face. "Not our idea, Colonel," he said. "Not that we disagree. But the President brought you in himself. Looks like you're out of the doldrums at last."

As Carter followed Hawk to the front door he could hear the cheerful bass voice behind him. "Bloody good," it was rumbling over and over. "Bloody good."

One more day passed without much progress, except that Carter was feeling like his old self. The wound had healed completely and he'd been given clearance for active duty by the medics.

At Dupont Circle Hawk paced his office. Rupert Smith, Howard Schmidt, and Carter sat in silence while their superior broke new ground through the clouds of smoke he'd created in the past fifteen minutes. They'd kicked the job around from every angle and Hawk was summing it up in his own mind.

"I don't like it," Hawk finally said. "The Setzel woman is in place at the embassy. Our woman's in place, holed up in a nest of dissidents. Nick goes in as an agro specialist. How do you get your supplies in, Howard?''

"At Kivak it's no problem. We have agents within the Alaska Inuit and they trade back and forth with relatives on the Soviet mainland," he said, stroking his pipe and trying to fend off the cigar smoke. "For some reason, the Soviets think they're simple-minded just because they're native people. I can get cylinders of gas taken in by them—explosives, weapons, uniforms, almost anything we want.''

"What about Moscow?''

"The major who commands the marines has agreed to accept any uniforms Nick might need in Moscow as part of his diplomatic package.''

"I don't like it," Hawk repeated. "If you can infiltrate Lumumba, the kids could be hostile. You can't pack them all in the embassy, even if you can get them to move. The ambassador can't take that kind of heat. Then we have the Spetsnaz camp. The kids are sure to be pro-Soviet by that time and word of your activity at Lumumba will have reached them. Last, the Kivak thing has possibilities, but by then they'll be on to you and the place will be like a hornet's nest.''

"Maybe we should drop the first two and go for the one with the best chance of success," Smith offered.

"That leaves God knows how many kids stranded in the Soviet Union. *Our* kids. We've got to give them a chance.''

"What do you think the odds are, Nick?" Schmidt asked.

"I'm not getting into guessing games. I'll know better when I'm on site. I'd like to get out of here tomorrow.''

"I don't want to rush this," Hawk said. "What about the unknown factor, Alice Hodgson? We might want her to go in with you.''

"I still think she'd be a liability. You don't go through their program and come out clean," Carter insisted.

"Let's see if Dr. Wilde agrees with you," Hawk suggested. He keyed in seven digits to a clean phone at Langley, and switched over to his speakerphone.

"Dr. Wilde? This is David Hawk. We may have to move soon. Will your patient be with us?"

"I don't see why not. Somehow she's managed to maintain control. I'd say she's true blue. Or should I say red, white, and blue?"

"I don't see how that's possible, Doctor," Carter spoke up. "Not after the program we've heard described."

"I'd stake my reputation on it."

Carter knew he was fighting a losing battle. Hawk knew as well as anyone that Carter was staking his life on her loyalty, not just his reputation. They talked for a few more minutes and disconnected after making arrangements for her delivery to an AXE safe house that afternoon.

"All right. We take off tomorrow. The Hodgson woman goes with me. You'll have to provide papers for her, Howard. Make her my secretary."

"That's it?" Hawk asked, looking from one face to another.

"No. The Hodgson woman and I both go into Howard's makeup shop this afternoon. I want her hair short and black. Add a birthmark to her face with dye. Her clothes should add thirty pounds. I want her teeth changed somehow."

"She'll raise hell," Smith warned.

"It wouldn't hurt her to make a few sacrifices for her country," Carter grunted. "If she goes with me, she's going to be unrecognizable to anyone she might have met in Moscow.''

The takeoff from Dulles International was uneventful. Carter was Philip Rolfe, an agricultural expert, and Alice Hodgson was Jane Dalton. Howard Schmidt had performed the transformation on her as Carter had asked, and Alice had not objected as he'd expected. Her acquiescence made Carter all the more suspicious. If she were just your average college student, she'd have balked at having her teeth discolored and capped unattractively. But this one had been given the most complete training courses available. She knew how to kill in a hundred ways. How could she have kept her own identity on the one hand, and been passive enough to suffer the physical changes he'd insisted on? It just didn't compute. Dr Kevin Wilde might just have made the blunder of his life.

Carter's dark hair was now silver, the lines of his face and his cheekbones were accented by expertly applied makeup and he wore black-framed eyeglasses with tinted lenses. Carter thought he looked like an aging, somewhat weatherbeaten Clark Kent.

''Tell me about Lumumba,'' he said. ''Describe the whole place.''

They were in first class, in seats three and four, against the forward bulkhead of the aircraft. A half-dozen small windows showed them the pale blue sky ahead and the odd wisp of cloud. It was a Lufthansa 747 that would take them to Frankfurt. The seats had been selected to isolate them. When Alice had to go to the bathroom, one of the attendants, an AXE agent, managed to keep an eye on her. She searched the washroom after Alice was finished.

"I'd like to go over more of the details," Carter told her when they'd been in the air a couple of hours. "How did you get to Lumumba?"

"We were taken inside by truck. I didn't see anything. Our compound was separate from the others. We were kept together all the time."

"For your whole induction and indoctrination?"

"The whole time."

"How long was the training?"

"I told you. It depended on if you were smart. At the end of each course, the smart ones would be moved on to another school."

"I don't see how they managed to integrate them when they were coming and going like that."

"They didn't."

"Didn't what?"

"I must have told you. When we came in by truck, we were it. They never tried to run different classes simultaneously."

Carter thought about it for a moment. "You didn't mention that. It makes one hell of a difference."

"I don't see why."

He didn't supply the answer but countered with another question. "Can we find out when the last group arrived?"

"I can bribe a guard."

"Good. That's our first task. Find out when the last group arrived." The plan was beginning to crystallize.

At Frankfurt, they transferred to an Aeroflot flight. It was an old Tupoluv 154 in need of a complete redecorating. Vinyl covering was peeling from the walls. The ceilings were mottled with water stains, and the smell of the washrooms was apparent in the cabin. What was worse, if Carter's ears were working at their superb best, the mechanical maintenance of the craft left a lot to be desired.

Alice slept most of the way. At Vnukova Airport they were to be met by an embassy car but none was apparent. Carter dragged Alice with him, bags and all, to the circle of telephone booths attended by a matron who would have been ugly even if she'd been a man.

Carter reached the embassy car pool and was told all the cars were out. If they would take the bus to the central terminal, a car would pick them up there, guaranteed.

Carter was too experienced to miss the implication. The CIA chief of station in Moscow was ticked off and was making life miserable for the interlopers. Right. They'd get that straightened out.

A car was waiting at the central terminal and the driver was the next thing to a deaf–mute. Carter didn't start his war with the driver. It was the station chief he had to straighten out.

He kept a close watch on Alice Hodgson. She had perked up when they touched down on Soviet soil. Why? Was her adrenaline flowing as his was? Was it for the same reason, or was her reaction one of returning home?

At the embassy, Carter expected the treatment normally given someone like an agro expert and that was what he got. They were led to connecting drab bedrooms and left to fend for themselves. Each room was equipped with a small desk and an embassy directory.

Carter locked the outer doors and pocketed the keys. He picked up one of the embassy directories and perused the names. One stood out like a beacon. The cultural attache was one Terry Crisp, known to Carter as a hard-nosed bastard who hated AXE with a passion. He dialed the number.

"Mr. Crisp's office."

"Tell him Nick Carter wants to talk to him—*now*!"

"I'm afraid I can't do that."

"Either you tell him or I drag my secretary through all the halls of this miserable place, in handcuffs, to his office. You got that?"

"What the hell is this, Carter?" Crisp came on the line.

"Send one of your people to stay with my secretary, and I'll be in your office in five minutes."

"You don't trust your own damned secretary?"

"I'll explain. Just do it."

Carter was in Crisp's office in the basement of the building within minutes. It was part of a small complex completely surrounded by a lead shield on all sides. Fresh air was fed in by special ducts.

"How much has Lynch told you?" he asked first.

"Just to cooperate."

"So what's the problem? Can't you follow orders for once?"

"You know the problem. I hate your guts."

"Look, Terry. The President has given this absolute top priority. Fred Lynch and Joe Cronyn are working hand in glove with my boss on this. The CJCS is in this up to his ass. The President himself suggested we get Delta Force into part of it. Doesn't that tell you something?"

"Holy shit! What's going on?"

Carter told him the story from the beginning, leaving out only insignificant details. The telling took a half hour. At the end of it, Crisp sent out for fresh coffee and sat back, more relaxed.

"Okay. So we bury the hatchet for now. I've got four kids myself. I'm in on this all the way."

"Lynch mentioned Sue Setzel. He cover that with you?"

"She'll be available soon, maybe tomorrow."

"I've got someone like her on our team."

"Frances Miner."

Carter scowled at the news. Frannie was supposed to be under deep cover, working with a large group of dissidents.

"I know," Crisp said. "I wouldn't have twigged to her, but we've been keeping an eye on the bunch she runs with and she was the extra piece of the puzzle. She had to be one of yours."

"Thank God the KGB isn't as observant."

"Don't bet on it."

"My real problem is the one upstairs. She's a graduate of the program. We pulled her in back home. Your Dr. Kevin Wilde has convinced everyone stateside that she's unaffected by their program."

"And you don't agree."

"Would you?"

"It's got to be a crock. I'll have her watched."

"What do you know about Lumumba?" Carter asked.

"Out in the boonies where they've got room to maneuver and play their war games."

"You know where?"

"Yeah."

"What about the one in town?"

"What one in town?" Crisp asked, putting his feet on the desk. He was a man running to fat, obviously more accustomed to desk duty than sweating or freezing in the field.

"The woman we picked up is called Alice Hodgson back home. She'll be Jane Dalton, my secretary, here," Carter explained. "She tells me they brought her to a building here they called Lumumba. Some kind of compound she never saw and another for the kids.''

"New."

"Can't be. It looks like this program's been going on for a few years."

"Shit! I should have known about it."

"Come on, Terry. You can't be expected to know everything. Did you get the packages sent for me?" he asked, changing the subject.

"In storage. I'll have them sent to your room."

"And I'll need a car."

"Got an old Yugo. Best I can do."

"No good. I'm going to visit Lumumba tonight as a major from the Inspector General's office. I'll have to arrive in at least an old Zil."

"Sorry, pal. Lots of majors would be pleased with the Yugo."

Carter didn't feel the problem big enough to make an issue. "When can I have Setzel?"

"Soon as she's free, maybe tomorrow."

"Where's the cafeteria? I'll meet her there at noon."

Crisp gave directions. "Where are you going to change into the major's uniform? Not on my turf, that's for sure."

"I'll need one of your safe houses while I'm here."

"Come on, Carter. You know I almost have to kill to get a small house or an apartment in this town."

"Just think about all the brass back home who expect you to cooperate with me," Carter said with a leering grin.

"Now I know why I hate you, you bastard. It's the goddamned clout. You bastards always have the clout. Okay. Jesus! You've got the safe house. But don't blow it."

Carter carried the heavy bundles to the third-floor bedrooms and relieved Crisp's guard.

"What's that?" Alice asked.

"Help me rip them open. One of them is for you. Let's try them on."

She knew without being told that the lieutenant's uniform was for her. With no modesty, she peeled to the buff and pulled on the course men's underclothes and the rest of the uniform. Carter was preoccupied with his own uniform but couldn't help noticing the body on the woman. It was about as perfect as God ever created. Not the body of a model or a Miss America, but the body of a courtesan, a few pounds more than the women who earned big money being photographed. Given the red hair and the green eyes, she'd have driven any man mad.

The pants and shirt in place, he reached to the bottom of the package for a special item. He took the front off the radio-cassette player that had served him through the years, and withdrew his 9mm Luger with some feeling. He'd had the gun for a long time. He could put eleven shots in a circle the size of a quarter nine times out of ten. In his younger days he'd affectionately called the gun Wilhelmina and the name still came to mind each time he saw her after an absence. He strapped the sling to his left shoulder and slung Wilhelmina under his left armpit.

Hugo was also packed in the radio. A long, thin stiletto that Carter could wield or throw with equal expertise, the knife had seen more action than most kitchen knives. He strapped the chamois sheath to his right forearm where he could flick it to his palm in an instant.

Last, Carter extracted a small round object from the radio case. It was larger than a walnut and smaller than a lime, a small gas bomb he'd dubbed Pierre in memory of a long-lost comrade. The gas in it was lethal. Sometimes he carried one that was meant to slow down an enemy, but this one was marked for dealing death. He dropped his pants and taped it high on his inner thigh.

In her uniform, Alice watched him. "The famous Killmaster arms himself," she said simply. "I don't suppose you've got something to fill my holster."

"Before we leave. When we know each other better, I might even give you some ammo—I *might*."

# SEVEN

The apartment was one of a half dozen on the top floor of a new building on Trubnikovsky Prospekt. Thousands of Muscovites would have done almost anything for such a place. Carter didn't know how Crisp had swung the deal and didn't want to know. It was intended for the privileged. Luckily, it was within walking distance of the embassy.

Alice Hodgson and Carter drove the old Yugo in a roundabout route to the apartment and lugged their bulky packages up four flights of stairs. The apartment building had no daily supervision, no old hag whose job it was to spy on the tenants. And most of the occupants were out to work. They heard no children at play, no vacuum cleaners, and smelled no borscht cooking.

The uniforms fitted perfectly. Carter helped Alice pad her shoulders and do what she could to disguise her figure. They removed all her makeup and shaded in a faint five o'clock shadow. The short dark hair, the port wine birthmark on her face, and the irregular tobacco-stained teeth changed her to resemble many of the average young lieutenants in the capital. Not many had the Don Johnson look.

Carter looked magnificent as the major. With the insignia of the Inspector General's office and a haughty attitude, he looked the part.

"Are you ready for this?" he asked, still not convinced that the illustrious CIA doctor was right about her.

"I don't even know what we're going to do."

He hadn't shared more than a few sentences with her about his plans since she'd been cleared by Dr. Wilde. "The uniforms give us an advantage," he told her. "We are from the Inspector General's office. I am Major Anatoly Marchenko. You are my assistant, Lieutenant Ivan Sokol. We're going to the new Lumumba school. You've got that?"

"Nothing wrong with my memory, Major. Why not pass me off as a woman? The Soviets aren't exactly chauvinists."

"Because you were a woman when you were here."

"I was a child. A freckle-faced innocent."

"I wanted a complete change. You look the part. Keep your voice in a low key. Better still, don't talk any more than you have to."

"And just what are we going to do?"

Carter studied the woman as he flipped a Soviet cigarette from his pack. She held out her hand. He lit both cigarettes. "This is just a recon. We'll take our first look at the place and make some evaluations."

"*Your* first look at the place. I'll never forget it."

"Let's be straight about this, Lieutenant. You're here because Dr. Wilde thinks you managed to get through their program without being converted. If he's wrong, you're accomplishing what Nancy Bell couldn't." He stood in front of her, looking into her face, locking onto her gaze. "If you cross me, I'll kill you, even if I have to go down."

"I know that. And it pisses me off that I'm a god-damned volunteer and you think I'm a traitor."

"So long as we understand each other."

"Okay. What happens next?"

"I assume you know your way around Moscow. We've both got driving permits in our identity kits."

"Where to?"

"Direct to Lumumba. You come in with me but try to say as little as possible."

"I wonder if old Borodin is still there," she said, as if thinking aloud, as they left the apartment.

"The commandant? My information confirms that. Small man, big ego."

"That's him, the bastard. He whipped me personally once."

"Keep your feelings off your face, Lieutenant Sokol. You've got to play the role of junior officer to the hilt. You got that?"

She didn't answer. Instead she moved around to the passenger side and held the door open for him. She was familiar with the little car, a popular model in the Soviet copied from the Italian Fiat.

Alice Hodgson, unrecognizable as the ravishing university student, drove with confidence north on Kachalova Street to the outer ring that circled the city, then turned right and south toward Tsvetnoy Boulevard. The new Lumumba complex filled a block across the ring from Tsvetnoy.

The visit was a total surprise to Borodin. Carter and Alice walked through the Lumumba compound with impunity and landed at the door of his office as he was chewing out a woman in an olive-green uniform and the shoulder boards of a newly commissioned lieutenant. He turned to scowl at the intrusion and found himself looking into the stern eyes of an impressive silver-haired major of the dreaded Inspector General's office.

"It's been a long time, Captain," Carter said, his expression inscrutable.

"It's always an honor, Major. You won't find anything out of order here."

"I'm sure. But we all have our responsibilities to the state."

"Just so."

"I am Major Marchenko. My assistant is Lieutenant Sokol."

Alice saluted, stood two paces behind Carter, and remained in that approximate position for the entire tour. She'd obviously seen inspections before, just as Carter had used the ruse before.

"They tell us so little of the details, Captain. I got this call just this morning. How many do you have in residence?"

"Twenty. We never have more than thirty and never less than fifteen."

"We'll have a look at them, Captain," Carter said, steeling himself for the contact. "But I'll have a word with my aide first."

He moved Alice off to one side and whispered to her in Russian. "This might be rough. Are you prepared?" It was the kind of warning a superior might have given a subordinate in any army unit, but it held special significance to them.

She squared her shoulders. "I know what to expect better than you. My face is going to be like a rock. Don't worry."

They were led into a kind of gymnasium. Twenty girls and boys wore tank tops and shorts and were forced to run around the outer perimeter until they dropped. Some were on the floor, panting, guards standing over them, shouting at them in Russian.

"They understand our language?" Carter asked.

"These are new recruits. We shipped out graduates last week."

Carter tried to hide his exultation. The feeling was weird. He mourned the plight of the newcomers, American kids in the process of torture of a kind, but he gloried in the fact that they were still not broken and would be eager to leave.

"Show me their sleeping quarters, Captain. I'd like to see their bathing facilities, the whole installation," Carter said imperiously. "This is an important project. I cannot stress that enough."

"I understand, Major. I take my work seriously," the small man replied. He was not cowed and he was not subservient. Obviously he knew he did his job well, and as an American it made Carter's blood boil. He wondered if Alice was going through the same inner turmoil and decided she had to be.

The boys' dormitory was spotless, every bunk as tightly made as those in many American military establishments. They'd accomplished much with these kids in a week. The showers were spotless. A ten-year-old was swabbing down the white tile floor. He moved off to one side, terrified at the sight of Carter's uniform.

"There are two sets of showers, Captain?" Carter asked.

"Just the one. We keep the sexes segregated, of course. No teen-age pregnancies here. Not like in the decadent imperialist West."

Carter glanced at Alice but her expression was blank. She had not made a move to reveal his identity. And she was not allowing her feelings to show. So far, he was winning.

"The kitchens, Captain," he ordered.

The kitchen was small but spotless, all the tables and stoves in stainless steel, the pots hanging in rows from a center work area, all gleaming as if brand-new.

Carter pulled a note pad from his pocket and scribbled a few words in Russian. He replaced the pad and turned toward the door.

"You will have a vodka with me?" Borodin asked, knowing the inspection was finished.

Carter pulled the pad from his pocket and made another entry. "That is not permitted," he said tersely as he led the way to the front door. "I will be back in a few days. You will not be notified," he told the quaking captain. "Some of these children might have to be examined by our experts."

"But this has not happened—"

"A new policy. You question the wisdom of the Inspector General, comrade?"

"Never, Major. We are at your disposal."

"That, Captain, is the most astute statement you've made today."

Alice held the door open for him and they drove way, merging into the traffic of the ring. "You were a real bastard. I almost laughed, but it was just too sad, you know?"

"I know." A hard knot had formed in the Killmaster's stomach. Kids. Twenty kids. American kids. His heart went out to them. When the time came, the people who ran Lumumba would be treated harshly. Not just for the ones he'd seen today, but for all the kids they'd processed over the years.

At the apartment, Carter pulled off his tunic and was about to pour himself a scotch when he heard her moaning behind him. She was just standing there, shaking like a leaf, her hands to her face. While he watched, she went to her knees, her head bent as if in supplication.

He went to her, picked her up, and placed her on the bed. For the time being he covered her, greatcoat and all, with a couple of blankets from his bed. He went to the bathroom where, miracle of miracles, he found a modern bathtub and a full tank of hot water. These places were definitely for the privileged. At that moment, despite their differences, he blessed Terry Crisp for his ingenuity.

He returned to the bedroom, pulled the covers from her, and removed all her clothing as gently as possible. He carried her, naked and unprotesting, to the waiting bath. He'd produced as much foam as possible with the harsh soap he'd found, and he eased her into the hot bubble bath.

Alice's only reaction was a small gasp as the hot water hit her and later a sigh as she settled into the sudsy cocoon.

Carter had a lot of thinking to do. How the hell was he going to get twenty kids out of the complex? That was a big group. How was he going to get them out inconspicuously? Crisp? No. It had to be something else. Frannie Miner. She was one of theirs. It would have to be her.

While Alice was soaking, he changed into the clothes he'd worn on the plane and drove back to the embassy as Philip Rolfe, the agro expert. He parked with a number of agency cars and made sure the watching KGB got a good look at his face.

Crisp was busy with an agent but stopped to talk to Carter. "How'd it go?" he asked.

"Soft probe. Got the lay of the land—and some luck."

"Glad someone has luck in this place," he muttered, pulling a bottle of scotch and two chipped mugs from a bottom drawer. "What happened?"

"Normal inspection. Found out the kids have been there for only a week."

"Carter, you'd fall in a shithouse and come out—"

Carter held up a hand in protest, then he held up his mug and proposed a toast. "To Lady Luck. She doesn't show up often in this racket, but when she does, look out."

They clinked mugs and tossed back the scotch. It burned all the way down and made Carter feel better than he had in a long time.

"How'd the Hodgson woman take it?"

"Like a trooper. She was as good as anyone could want, right up until we were back at the apartment. Then she fell apart."

"It had to be tough on her."

"Damned tough. I left her soaking in a hot bath. I still don't know how you managed a place like that."

"We don't talk about it, okay? But you left her alone?"

"She's all right. And if she's not, she could tip them any time. So why not leave her alone?"

"Maybe. If I could think like that I probably wouldn't have ulcers."

"Ulcers and scotch?" Carter asked. "God preserve me from a job like yours. By the way, did you get my message to Frannie?"

"She's anxious to talk to you."

"No more than I. Where do I get her?"

"The boiler room of the Moscow Hotel."

"What . . . ? You're kidding."

"The chief engineer at the hotel is one of her people. Not even the hotel manager dares to step into the chief's domain."

Carter set down his mug and roared with laughter, startling Crisp. Frannie Miner was too much. He hadn't seen her in years and looked forward to the reunion.

"You think it's too late to pay her a visit now?"

"I'd leave it until morning," Crisp advised. "They watch anyone who leaves here like a hawk, particularly at this hour."

"Then it's back to the apartment for Philip Rolfe. If anyone asks, I'm doing the tourist bit for a few days before I drop into the Ministry of Agriculture. With any luck, this part of it will be cleared up in a few days."

He left Crisp in his lead-lined room, protected from the intense Soviet effort to break his security, and headed for his old car.

It had turned much colder. The interior of the car was like a refrigerator. The motor barely caught and he turned into the newly fallen snow. He could have walked to the apartment, but it was bitter cold, and he wanted to maintain his role as the decadent American.

Alice was in the bed, covered with only one blanket. Her lush figure was outlined by the thin covering. She looked calm and relaxed now, a very different young woman from the one that had broken down earlier. Her green eyes were clear and bright. The smile she flashed for him was unreserved.

"You did very well," he said simply, feeling deadly tired. The strength and stamina he was noted for had not yet completely returned, and the knife wound ached occasionally.

"Until I got back here."

"None of us is made of steel, Alice. You were there for me when it counted."

"You want to make love to me?"

The question was so unexpected, he was stunned for a moment. A man who'd loved many women and who was usually a target for their passion, he was shocked by the abrupt offer. Now he knew how the oldest excuse in the world had originated: "I'm too tired tonight."

But his libido didn't fail him entirely. He stripped out of his clothes and joined her in bed. He held her tenderly without making any overtures. "Do you need me?" he asked.

"Not really. I was . . . hell, I don't know . . . I was relaxed, feeling like I'd conquered my fears, thought I could do something for you."

He kissed her on the cheek and lay on his side of the bed. "If it's going to happen, it'll happen," he said. "What did you think of the visit today?"

"Well, Borodin hasn't changed."

"Tell me how many people are employed there."

"Borodin, an assistant, half a dozen guards, a cook, and a kitchen helper."

"That's it?"

"Yes."

"Ten people. You're sure?"

"Yes. Why?"

"Details I have to know. There's another part to that facility. Did they ever have contact with you?"

"Never. Mostly Middle Eastern terrorists."

"That helps."

She was quiet for a long time. "You're going to get them out, aren't you?"

"Yes."

"How?"

So it had come down to the moment of truth. If he told her his plan he could be killed, the plan would fail, and AXE would lose Frannie Miner and her contact with the dissidents.

She was good. She was very good. Maybe she was the best agent the KGB had ever produced . . . or . . . or she was Alice Hodgson, the girl they'd tried and failed to turn into a robot.

How the hell could he be sure? Dr. Wilde was convinced and he was the expert, but . . .

"Go to sleep," he sighed, rolling over. "We've got a long day ahead of us tomorrow."

She slid across to mold herself to him, warm, soft and inviting.

"You still don't trust me," she said. "What do I have to do?"

"Give it more time," he said, sleepily. "See you in the morning."


The Moscow Hotel was too far from the apartment to walk. Carter woke Alice and told her to stay in the apartment until he came back. He'd have left a note, but he didn't know if she could read Russian and he wasn't about to leave one in English. "I've got to see some people," he said. "You can be thinking about the rescue. It will be your job to reassure the kids while I deal with the others. You'll be in a Russian uniform and you have to convince them to follow you. Think about that while I'm gone."

He parked the small car in the front of the hotel and

headed for the main bank of elevators. He rode the elevators for about ten minutes, getting off at different floors, riding to the food and beverage storage area below, finally finding a stairwell door leading to the boilers. No one followed him after the first five minutes.

He was challenged when he opened the door. The name of his friend was the password. "Frances," he said.

"Come," was all the giant in the oil-streaked coveralls said.

She was sitting at the chief's desk as if she owned the joint. "Nick!" she screamed at him, then came flying, her short blond hair moving from side to side as if alive. Her hazel eyes met his just before she wrapped her arms around his neck and she kissed him long and hard. They'd been lovers once, a long time ago, when they were much younger and more hot-blooded. Now they knew that if the opportunity came, it would be a bonus. If it did not, they had their memories, and those better than most.

"Hawk called me himself. Said I had to give you all the help I could. Tell me about it."

He gave her a quick rundown. "So I have to get the kids out of there and out of the country," he told her.

She thought about the problem for a long time. He watched her while he smoked. She was a trained agent, one of the best. He could use all the help she could dream up.

"I can get them from Moscow to Estonia. I've got contacts on the border. How many are we talking about?"

"Twenty. Give or take one or two."

"The problem is how to get them out of Lumumba and into my hands."

"I've thought of that. Are your people willing to take some risks?"

"Like what?"

"A subway ride. A mad dash into the American embassy. We'd have to release them in a couple of days, of course. An interrogation would follow."

"That's it?"

"Not as bad as before *glasnost*. But you never know."

"I think they will risk it. But I'd like to speak to Hawk first."

"You got a radio?"

"A clean telephone to the American embassy and a patch. No problem."

It was the small hours of the morning in Washington when they reached Hawk at his apartment, but he sounded as if he'd been up and going over some files. Carter could never remember when he'd ever caught AXE's founder and chief sounding like someone just roused from sleep.

After the usual preliminaries Frannie asked for help. "I can get the kids into Estonia but I'd need a pickup somewhere outside a town called Nisi."

"No chance of you getting them out to one of our subs?"

"No way. I need helicopters enough to pick up twenty kids. Figure the average weight at a hundred and twenty pounds. Two troop carriers, something like the old Hueys they used in 'Nam could do it."

"What are the defenses like at Nisi?"

"Minimal. That's why I use it."

"I'll talk to the CJCS. He's in on this. Two long-range troop carriers could make it from Sweden with extra tanks."

"I'm pulling this off in two days," Carter said. "Late at night, about midnight day after tomorrow."

"I'll take the kids off his hands and have them in

Estonia late the next night if we don't run into trouble. That's midnight, two days after tomorrow, Estonian time.''

"Set up the usual AXE recognition signal from the ground.''

"Will do, sir. Better tell them to make a second run twenty-four hours later if we don't make it on time.''

"You sure you can do this, Nick?''

"Better than fifty percent. Worth going for.''

"Anything else?'' Hawk asked.

They told him about the dissidents and the embassy.

"My God! That should shake them up. I'll get to the President as soon as he wakes and get back to you. Be available in three hours, Miner. I can't see a hitch, but this one's his call to make.''

"Tell Howard to send me two small gas bombs, one uniform, colonel, KGB, and a makeup kit,'' Carter requested. "Tell him to make up a uniform for the Hodgson girl—make it for a female KGB captain.''

"Anything else?''

"I've got my radio, so I'll call in the computer by satellite when I want supplies for Kivak.''

They were about to sign off when Carter thought of something else. "I don't have my small case of drugs. Send it along too.''

"Will do. Take care of yourselves.''

They signed off.

"He didn't ask about the Hodgson girl,'' Frannie said.

"She was cleared by the CIA's top man in chemical substance use and abuse. Hawk wouldn't ask about her. He'd expect us to tell him if she's out of line. And I asked for a uniform for her for the next part of the job.''

"I guess you're right. Are you sleeping with her yet, you bum?''

"No."

"How old is she?"

"I don't know. Twenty . . . twenty-one, something like that."

"Jesus!" Frannie said, shaking her head. "Sometimes I think there's no God, you know?"

# EIGHT

"I'd like to meet your people," Carter told Frannie. "I'd like to tell them myself what they're getting into."

"You don't trust me?"

"I'd like to gauge their reaction, okay?"

She led him to a larger chamber that was immaculate. Two huge boilers stood majestically in the center of the room, painted yellow, connected to a forest of pipes jutting out in all directions. The floor was cement painted a light green and spotless. The whole place showed the pride the chief engineer took in his profession.

In a cleared area behind the boilers, hidden by the framework that was part of the installation, about fifty men and women sat in a circle, a brute of a man sitting in the middle, reading poetry. Carter wasn't familiar with contemporary Soviet poetry, but he listened intently: the imagery was good, the rhythms original, and the flow of words, each an extension of the other, was like a platoon of soldiers, each dependent on the other for its existence. The message was crystal clear: *glasnost* was good, but it was only the beginning of freedom and democracy.

"This is my friend, Nick Carter," Frannie interrupted. "He's the best agent in my organization and he has a problem."

"If we can help a friend of Comrade Miner's . . ." the big man said, waving his arms to form the group into a half circle.

Carter explained the Soviet use of American kids to foster their spy network in the United States. The group was incensed.

"What can we do to help, Comrade Carter?"

Again he explained what he'd told Alice. "Your part will be to assemble at the closest Metro station to the Lumumba complex."

"That will be Taganskaya," one of the dissidents offered. "I'm a cleaner on the subway line."

"You will wait on the platform and when you see me with the twenty kids, you will take the next train."

"What time would that be?" the same man asked.

"Midnight," Carter replied.

"They run about every fifty minutes at rush hour. Maybe seventy minutes at midnight."

"Thank you, comrade," Carter interjected, but the man was not finished.

"The last train is at one in the morning. Don't change your plan for later."

"Thank you, comrade. What I propose is that we ask twenty of you, the smallest, to dress as the kids would dress, and take the next train. When your train arrives at the American embassy—"

"That's Smolenskaya Station," the enthusiastic subway employee offered. "But may I speak further, comrade?"

"Certainly."

"At Taganskaya Station, I know of a large closet in which we keep cleaning equipment. You know how the KGB patrols the stations. Instead of waiting around and bringing attention to ourselves, we can wait in the supply room and watch you board the train," he said, looking around at the group, gesturing with his arms. "Besides, it would look unusual for us to wait for a train, for you to board the children, and for us to pass up the train and take the next."

"Thank you, comrade," Carter said sincerely. "That was a problem that bothered me. So you will decide on the twenty who will participate, hide in the supply room at about ten minutes to midnight, and take the train that follows ours."

"You were going to tell us what we do at the American embassy, Comrade Carter?" one of the women asked.

"This is the difficult part," Carter told them. "The embassy will be expecting you. If we ride on with the children to another station and head out of the country, the authorities will assume that the group in the embassy are the children," he said, waiting a moment for them to digest the thought. "Since Soviet officials will have been caught in a horrendous crime, they won't know what to expect. They will be meeting night and day to write up denials for the international press. The ambassador will not issue a statement until the children are safely out of the country."

They sat around him, their faces a mixture of surprise, elation, and concern. Many had questions on the tips of their tongues but waited.

"You will be released from the embassy a few at a time. The authorities will question you and you will tell them that you were asked to help with a cultural program. We will provide you with false documents of authority from your Ministry of Cultural Affairs. Hopefully, no penalties will result.''

The small subway employee raised his hand.

''What is it, comrade?'' Carter asked.

''I'd like to volunteer.''

Immediately all hands were raised and they started to shout among themselves. Frannie Miner stepped in and calmed them. ''This part does not concern Mr. Carter. Are there any questions before he goes?''

''Yes,'' a woman at the back asked.

''What is it, comrade?'' Frannie asked.

''Surely the KGB have a program that is more complicated than the Lumumba training. Can we help further?''

Carter pulled Frannie off to one corner and whispered. ''I can't reveal my plans to this many of your people. They could be infiltrated.''

''They are not. I'd bet my life on it. Besides, if they are, you'll be dead at Lumumba and the rest is history.''

He thought about it for a moment, then turned to the assembly. ''A good question, comrade,'' he told the woman. ''But the next phase is miles from here, halfway to Leningrad.''

''We have affiliate groups all over the country. We can call in thousands if you need them.''

Carter was surprised. Rupert Smith should have known about this. The CIA should have known about so much sympathetic help. And the revelation was a testimony to the faith they had in Frannie.

''Did you know about this?'' he whispered to her.

''I'm just beginning to catalogue it. I was going to send a report to Washington by diplomatic courier next week.''

''What about Terry Crisp?''

"Screw Crisp."

He turned back to the group, a broad smile on his face. "This could be the best news I've had since I arrived. I'll talk it over with Frannie and decide if we can use your organization. Thank you, comrade."

The woman waved and smiled from the back of the group. Carter knew that luck was running in his direction and as a gambler from way back, he was going to play his winning streak to the end.

"You've got all you need for now," he told Frannie. "When you're finished at the embassy, come back here. I'll call you."

Carter was on the first floor with Captain Borodin and his staff. Some of them had been awakened by the eleven o'clock surprise visit. Alice was on the second floor in the boys' dormitory. She shook the biggest of the boys awake. He jumped as if he'd been scalded, was out of bed in an instant and standing at attention.

"I want you to awaken the other boys quietly and wait for me. I'm going to get the girls," she told him quietly in English.

The girls were alert more quickly and began to chatter among themselves.

"Quiet!" Alice ordered. "You will follow me," she commanded, keeping her voice low.

When they were all in the boys' dormitory, she told them to sit on the bunks and pull the blankets around them. The inside temperature must have been about fifty degrees.

"This is the uniform of an officer of the Inspector General's command. My major is downstairs now, busy with the staff." Her voice was low and still modulated to imitate a male member of the military. "What I am going to tell you will be such a shock that you must hold your hands over your mouths to keep from making a noise,'' she went on.

Some of the girls started to cry, along with the youngest of the boys.

"Don't cry. It is happy news, but I don't want you to cry out," she said in her normal voice.

The sudden change got their attention. Some of them put their hands over their mouths in preparation for the surprise, and the woman's heart went out to them.

"Listen carefully," she continued in her own voice. "I was one of you ten years ago—right here—in one of the bunks in the girls' room. The training was long and difficult. When all the children were trained, we were sent back home. But by that time they were spies of the Soviet government," she said, looking around at the twelve boys and eight girls.

"But they did not succeed with me. I am back here now to take you home . . ."

She was interrupted by an outburst, despite her warnings.

"Quiet!" she shouted in Russian. If the sound drifted down the stairs it would seem natural.

"I told you to be quiet," she repeated in English, her voice low. "Since the American government found out about you, they sent my colleague and me to get you out."

Hands shot up as if they were in a classroom.

"Wait until I'm finished, please. Okay?"

The hands went down and the young people continued to stare at her. It was a pitiful sight in those drab surroundings, but it was heartwarming at the same time. She saw courage there, and hope. Faces prematurely etched with worry lines glowed.

"Tomorrow at ten minutes to midnight I will come for you. You must be able to dress in five minutes and be ready to go out in the cold. Do you have clothes for the cold?"

"I thought you had been here," one of the boys said. "We didn't have warm clothes. It was summer."

"We have winter clothes," one of the girls offered.

"Then you will dress and as soon as you see me, you will be prepared to march out. We will march to the Moscow subway, my major in the lead, and we will get on the subway. Any questions?"

None of the children raised a hand.

"You must look as if you are obeying orders. You must act as you would if two army officers were taking you off to a dreadful place. Hang your heads. Look frightened."

"Where are you taking us?" one of the girls asked.

She was young and pretty. She looked so vulnerable that Alice was reminded of her time there. A tear coursed down the woman's cheek and she swiped it away angrily.

"We will ride the subway for a few stops, then we'll get off and be marched to a warehouse where a friend will put you in a truck. You will have to travel all night and all the next day. It will be cold. You will be given food and portable potties to use as toilets. You will not be able to stop for any reason. It will be very difficult. Questions?"

"Why are they doing this to us?" one of the youngest asked.

"They wanted you to grow up in their training camps and return home as spies, to do bad things and hurt your country."

"To hurt our own parents?"

"It's so hard to explain. You wouldn't even know

your parents by then. You'd have forgotten them.''

"But we'd never forget them," one of the older boys said.

"We don't have time for all the questions, children. Just one point. You must not give the slightest hint about any of this to anyone. Don't talk to each other about it. Try to look as unhappy as you've been the last few days. If they hear you talking, they might stop us from taking you home. Do you understand?''

"If you think we could tell, why come to us now?" one of the older girls asked.

"Good question. I've just told you what's going to happen to you. I thought you had to know.''

"What happens when we get out of the truck?" one of the boys asked.

"Two helicopters will pick you up and take you for a long ride. Then you will be safe and you can be flown home.''

She waited while they whispered among themselves but she was running out of time.

"Okay. I will repeat some things. You *cannot* talk about this. You *must* act like prisoners when we take you out. You *must* act the same as if someone like Captain Borodin was in charge when we are in the subway station and riding in the subway. I will turn you over to friends of mine when we leave the subway. You will be free to talk then.''

"What happens if someone talks?" the largest of the boys asked.

"Then my friend and I will probably die. You will never see your parents again.''

They were stunned into silence for a moment.

"We will not talk," the same boy assured her.

The smallest girl raised her hand.

"What is it?" Alice asked.

"Could you hug me like my mommy? Please?"

They came together tenderly and the others crowded around for a moment or two, all in one big circle, an embrace they all needed.

"Okay. Back to your beds and not a word," Alice said, raising herself to her full height.

When they were back in bed, she made the rounds and they were going back to sleep. She went into the washroom to check her appearance. Tears had run through the five o'clock shadow. She scrubbed her face and applied a new smudge of makeup.

As she prepared to leave, a huge sob built up in her but she struggled against her emotions and managed to hold it back. By the time she began to descend the stairs, she was back to normal, Lieutenant Ivan Sokol, resolute and ramrod straight.

On the way back to the apartment, Carter asked about the kids.

"They will do very nicely. I'm confident about this."

"I still don't think you were right in trusting the kids."

"I'm glad you let me talk with them. Tomorrow they will be like soldiers. I know. A kind of barracks-block loyalty springs up between them. They become survivors. Even after only one week I could see the inner spirit of the kids has already formed that bond.

"On the other hand, if I hadn't gone tonight and prepared them, tomorrow would be total confusion and fear. Anyone seeing them in the subway would be suspicious. You know Muscovites. They would have rushed to a telephone to get to the KGB."

"I hope to hell you're right. I've never seen twenty kids who could keep a secret for twenty-four hours," he said. "We won't have long to find out if you're right," he concluded, turning into their street and parking the small car.

"I've got you on a scrambled line with the ambassador," Ginger Bateman said over the intercom. "Line one."

"Franklin," Hawk said. "It's been a long time."

Franklin Walters and David Hawk had crossed paths many times through the years. It would have been impossible for them to avoid each other with Walters growing in stature in the diplomatic community, moving from one posting to another, and Hawk controlling agents in every part of the globe.

Walters was a dedicated man, a family man, and while he found Hawk's activities in his territory disturbing, he knew the work was a necessity.

"I've just been lucky, I guess."

"How much do you know about the job at Lumumba?"

"Crisp has filled me in. Terrible business," Walters said with emotion. "But I don't know how you plan to take them out."

"Carter will handle that. We don't want the KGB to pick them up right away. They apparently have a safe place for meetings, so they'll leave one or two at a time and make their way to their own place."

"What's the party line on publicity? I should have heard from my boss on this," Walters said.

"This is the President's baby. Your boss is in Geneva and the undersecretaries aren't in on it. He wants you to keep a lid on it."

"And if I'm called before the First Minister?"

"Our guess is they don't know what the hell to do. They've been caught with their hands in the cookie jar.

But if they're stupid enough to call you, deny, deny, deny."

"I will. This is one hell of a business, David. What about the rest of our kids?"

"Carter estimates they have about forty at a Spetsnaz camp between Moscow and Leningrad, and as many as a hundred at a last staging point not far from Alaska."

"But how is he going to get them out?"

"Don't underestimate Carter, Franklin. Just do all you can to help him."

"Crisp is a rigid type. What do you suggest?"

"I'll have Fred Lynch lean on him from here," Hawk said. "I've got a meeting with the President in a half hour. And I'll keep you posted."

"Bad business. I've never seen anything like it. Jesus, David! We've got to make this one work."

"It's all right, Franklin. I don't worry about anything I can't control. And I work like hell on anything I can. Right now I'm working overtime, okay?"

"Anything you want, David. Just ask."

Hawk put down the phone and thought about Carter in the middle of it. He'd be all right. He had a good feeling about this one—a good feeling.

Ginger Bateman stuck her head in the door. "Howard's out back in the car. You'll be late."

In the close to midnight traffic, they made it to the White House in less than fifteen minutes. They were met at the East Wing Lobby by a Secret Service agent who led them silently through a warren of corridors and down two flights of stairs to a room with walls three feet thick, reinforced with sheets of steel and lined with lead. It was a room used only for high-level meetings involving national security.

The President sat at the head of the table, casually

dressed in slacks and a cardigan. General Chris Farmer, the CJCS, was dressed as a twin, as if they had been golfing together. It was the first time Hawk had seen the general out of uniform. Fred Lynch was in a business suit as was Joe Cronyn. It appeared that only the men in intelligence had been working straight through.

"David called this meeting. I'm turning it over to him," the President said.

Hawk took his time, lit a cigar, and watched the smoke disappear though high-powered exhaust vents almost as fast as it left his mouth.

"I wanted you to start thinking of innovative ideas about the next two jobs," he started.

"Next two?" General Farmer asked, raising an eyebrow.

"I'm sorry. Guess I haven't had time to brief you all. The first phase is all but completed. Your choppers should find the kids at the rendezvous point within hours."

A general air of confidence filled the room as smiles broke out and the President congratulated Hawk.

"We've just started, really," Hawk said. "They are warned now, first by the Bell woman, then the navy kid, Branch Scott. We've pulled in a lot of their people. The Lumumba school has been penetrated and their newest batch of recruits have been spirited away. The Soviets are always paranoid. This must be sending them into orbit."

"Good. Excellent. It's about time we shook them up," the President said, putting his slippered feet on the table and leaning back, satisfied.

"Doesn't all this make it a lot tougher for your man?" Farmer asked.

"You've got that right. But if I wanted anyone in the

thick of this mess, it would be him," Hawk said, building a fire at the end of his cigar, itching to get up and pace but knowing this wasn't the place. "Here are some of the problems as I see them," he went on. "He's got to penetrate the Spetsnaz camp and evaluate the situation. He'll be asking us for help to knock them all out, including the kids. That's Howard's job. He'll be working on it. We'll need transport out of the area."

"Where is it?" the general asked.

"A place called Pestovo, about halfway between Moscow and Leningrad. You've got to get in, load up with about forty kids, and get out without air cover."

"You don't fool around, do you?" the general kidded.

"We've got to get those kids out," Hawk reiterated. "That's the objective. *All* the kids."

The President seemed about to interject a thought but changed his mind and sat back.

"Last, the Kivak evacuation is going to be a bitch. We've got the Delta people standing by. The commanding officer at Eielson Air Force Base in Alaska has to be briefed. We probably need a carrier on the north end of the Bering Sea."

"I'll be at Eielson myself," Farmer announced. "You need anything, you ask for me."

"One last thing—and I'm sure it's another challenge for Howard," Hawk said. "We've got to knock out all resistance when Carter flushes them all from underground. He'll come up with something. We'll keep you informed."

The President sat forward at this point, his elbows on the table. "I want all of those children home, gentlemen. I want every one of them. And I want to rub the Soviets' noses in this. Détente and *glasnost* are all well and good. But the one thing they respect is strength. If we pull this

off, we can blackmail them from Chuckchi to Vladivos-
tock and back.''

''What do we do with the kids when we get them
home?'' Joe Cronyn asked.

''We'll worry about rehabilitation when the time
comes,'' the President said, rising to his feet.

Hawk managed to grab Lynch's arm out in the hall
when he was taking off in a hurry. ''I didn't want to
mention it in there, Fred, but your man Crisp is becoming
a problem. I need your help.''

''Crisp can be rigid. What's the problem?''

''Like you said, rigid. We need some slack on this
one. Tell him to cooperate or else.''

''Or else what, David?''

''Or else you'll crawl all over him.''

''And if he doesn't respond?''

''Come on, Fred. You know your job. But if he doesn't
cool it in the next twenty-four hours, I'll have him put
out of action. We don't have room for petty jealousies
on this one.''

Fred Lynch squeezed Hawk's arm. ''I'll handle it,
David. It's too big for one man to screw up.''

# NINE

In the huge building on 16th Street in Washington, Ambassador Lubkov sat with Morotov and Tsarev. "When do you propose we report to Moscow?" he asked with a scowl.

"A few more days, comrade," Tsarev pleaded. It was his neck on the line for the Nancy Bell fiasco. Morotov would have to answer for the loss of the navy man, Branch Scott.

"They probably know about the FBI picking up many of our plants in the Pacific Northwest. Our comrades out there probably reported it right away," Lubkov warned. "Director Ruzimatov could be sitting back waiting to see how long it will take you to report."

"A couple of days can't hurt, comrade," Tsarev repeated. "By then we might have turned the tables on them."

"And if it gets worse?" Lubkov asked. "What if they already have interrogated their captives and are infiltrating right now?"

"Then we are dead men, all of us," Morotov responded glumly, reaching for the vodka bottle that had been his companion for the last few days.

Captain Valerian Borodin sat in his office alone. He was smarting under the pressure of the two inspections and was determined to do something about it. In his whole career, and he'd served under some very powerful men, no one had ever questioned his loyalty or ability.

Something was very wrong here. He'd inspected the new recruits that morning and they seemed different, less cowed, as if they knew something he didn't. He'd seen the attitude in the foolish expressions of religious people just before they were about to die, as if, by some miracle, someone was coming out of the heavens to scoop them up and take them from him. They'd whispered more than usual and been whipped for it. They were different. Could they . . . ?

It was preposterous, but maybe he should do something about it. The Inspector General's office was a possibility, but if he was wrong, he'd be in more trouble than he could handle.

He'd give it one more day.

The most feared man in the Soviet Union was not the First Minister. Yevgeny Popolov was a man to be feared as the head of state, a man with infinite power, but Boris Ruzimatov, who ran the KGB, was known as "the butcher," a sadist who had chosen an office in the old KGB building next to Lubyanka instead of the one used by his predecessors in the new building on the outer ring. Everyone knew why. Ruzimatov loved pain, was fascinated by watching prisoners scream under the most horrible torture he could devise, and the proximity to Lubyanka was to his liking.

A young colonel opened the door after knocking discreetly. "A call from our man in the northwest United States, Excellency," he said. The director liked to be called "Excellency." He'd been known to ship men off to the gulags for the simple act of forgetting the self-imposed title.

"What does he want?"

"He wouldn't tell me, Excellency. Said it was for you alone."

Ruzimatov pushed the lighted button on his phone. "What is it?" he asked. He never addressed an underling by name.

"It is further to the tragedy of last June, Excellency."

"You have learned whether the Americans suspect?"

"Not exactly, Excellency," the frightened voice came over the scrambled line. "We have been raided by their Federal Bureau of Investigation."

"Raided? You mean your headquarters?"

"No, Excellency. They somehow knew of some of our foster homes. More than a dozen families have been taken, including the candidates."

"Fools! You couldn't see this coming?" Ruzimatov bellowed. The kidnap plot had been his brainchild when he'd been a deputy director. It had earned him high honors and his present exalted position. The First Minister had taken credit for the idea, but most in authority knew who was the author. And now he was compromised. Even he would not be free from the wrath of those above him if the juvenile pipeline was broken.

"We had no suspicion that they knew of the locations."

"Something smells of bad fish here," Ruzimatov said

as if talking to himself. ''They would have to know something. One of the earlier candidates would have to have been unearthed and interrogated, something like that. But why haven't I heard from someone? One of my people is hiding something, sitting on something hoping to save his neck.''

He hung up in mid-thought, leaving the poor soul at the other end uncertain of his fate.

How much did they know? he asked himself. Were they already following up the trail after interrogating the people they'd taken in? It was the way that his mind worked, always torturing himself with doubts. He was like an Indian fakir lying on a bed of nails, always vulnerable to a weight suddenly being dropped on him.

Were his camps at home secure? Was Lumumba safe? Pestovo and Kivak? He looked at his watch. He had a late meeting with the First Minister. But he'd not discuss this news. Tomorrow he would call Lumumba. Tomorrow he would tighten security on all three camps.

He pulled a drawer open and reached for a bottle to give him courage. So they knew about the plan. He knew they would someday. But now? Why did it have to be now?

The guard at Lumumba recognized them but challenged them regardless. Imperiously, Carter waved his identification in front of the guard's nose. The frightened man glanced at it and didn't bother with Alice's papers at all.

Inside, at a quarter to midnight, Alice headed for the dormitories while Carter headed for Captain Borodin's office. The man wasn't there. The Killmaster went back to the guard and demanded to be taken to Borodin's sleeping quarters.

The place smelled of stale vodka and unwashed bodies. The captain snored in the bed, a teen-age boy on either side of him. The two youngsters sat up, frightened, and he waved them outside without a word.

Borodin sat up, wiping his eyes, then his body stiffened as he recognized the major at the foot of his bed. He looked for the boys and seemed relieved that they were no longer there.

"I told you I would be back," Carter said, his voice like the crack of a whip. "Get your pants on. We're going to your office."

The man scrambled for his pants and his boots. He was still pulling on a shirt while he followed Carter to his office.

"I want to see the whole staff here, at once," Carter demanded.

"Now see here . . ." Borodin started to say.

The Luger was in Carter's hand so fast that the Soviet official blinked.

"You will call all of your staff in here, or you are dead where you sit."

"This is highly irregular, Major."

"It is not in the least irregular, Borodin. Do you think I didn't see your abuse of the two young boys? Do you think we want to turn them into your kind?"

"You have no right—"

"I'll tell you what I have the right to do," Carter interrupted acidly. "I have the right, as an officer of the Inspector General's personal staff, to execute anyone of junior rank for an offense like the one I saw in your bedroom. Now call the rest of the staff in here—all of them!"

• • •

Above their heads, Alice had wakened all the children. They were standing around, excited, all holding back the urge to talk, all dressed for the cold outdoors.

"You must be absolutely quiet until we hear from my major. He is making sure that the way is clear for us to move downstairs and out into the night," she said, trying to keep her voice low. "Do you remember what I told you last night?"

"We are to look sad, hang our heads, but to march with you to the subway."

"That's right. I have a coin for each of you, five kopeks. You will see me deposit a similar coin in a slot and take a ticket. You will do the same and give it to the conductor when asked. Questions?"

None of them asked questions. God, they were brave, she thought. She'd forgotten how quickly she had assimilated, had learned to think clearly, to listen and react with speed. "Just so you will know, the subway is called the Metro and the stations have a large red *M* over each entrance. The stations are large and will be decorated with artwork. They are built with large columns holding up the roofs. They have panels of heroes decorating the walls. You will not look up or pay any attention to either the surroundings or the people around you. Is that clear?"

They all nodded.

"You will see only the feet of the person in front of you. We will all gather at the end of one car and not pay any attention to any of the other passengers."

She was interrupted by what could only have been a shot. The children jumped. Some began to cry.

"Quiet!" she hissed at them. "Now follow me in single file. We will go to the top of the steps and wait."

• • •

Carter stood with Wilhelmina in one of his greatcoat pockets. One by one the staff filed in, sleepy and grumbling. "Now the guards," he ordered.

Reluctantly Borodin pushed a button that connected him to all the guards. Before he could speak, he was looking into the 9mm barrel. Carter kept the gun between himself and the other members of the staff—the cook, his helper, and the newly commissioned female lieutenant.

"You will come to my office immediately," Borodin commanded, his voice not as confident as usual, but Carter was sure the guards would not notice.

Six soldiers entered one at a time, each with a Kalashnikov automatic rifle slung over his shoulder. Borodin seemed to perk up when he saw the guns.

"Put your weapons on the floor," Carter ordered, showing the Luger to the others for the first time.

"What is this, Major?" the mannish-looking female lieutenant asked.

"A new type of inspection, Lieutenant. This is a test of memory. As an example, how many children have passed through here? What is the total?"

"That will show up in the log, Major."

"Shut up, you fool!" Borodin said.

One of the soldiers went for the AK-47 rifle at his feet. Carter shot him in the head. The blood and brain matter splattered the men and women behind him. They screamed as the noise of the shot faded, wiped at the gore, and moved away from him, the specter of their own deaths shrouding them.

"The log, Lieutenant, please."

The woman didn't move. He pointed the Luger at her head. She pulled open a drawer and handed him a leather-covered book that was small enough to fit in his greatcoat pocket.

"How long have you all been here?" he demanded. "From the beginning?"

Most of them nodded.

"And you all knew that you were processing children to become robots?"

"But it was for the state," the cook protested. "We were proud to do it for the state."

"The state also hands out penalties," Carter responded. In a diversionary action, he swung the gun toward Borodin and shot him in the shoulder. While the others were preoccupied with the captain, he reached down for Pierre, stripped it from his inner thigh, took a deep breath, and tossed the activated bomb on the desk in front of the wounded captain.

While they stood, dumbfounded, not knowing what the major was doing, and still cowed by authority, Carter slipped out the door and locked it from the outside. Within seconds the occupants would be dead. For once the killing gave him pleasure. He'd have done the same to the people who ran Bergen-Belsen or any of Hitler's death camps.

At the top of the stairs, Alice and the children heard the second shot but didn't have time to think about it. Within seconds, Carter appeared at the bottom of the steps and waved them down.

They walked out of the building into a light snowfall. The long line, headed by the major and tailed by the lieutenant, drew the attention of the few who dared use the streets at that hour. Within minutes they were in the Metro station and heading down a long escalator to the train level. Alice had briefed Carter on the routine. He dropped the five-kopek piece in a slot and took a ticket. The children did the same, then resumed their meek demeanor, heads down, eyes regarding the feet of the child in front of them.

A draft of cold air built up from the black tunnel at the end of the platform as the approaching train pushed a wall of air in front of it like a giant piston. Within seconds of their arrival, the train rushed into the station, a steel juggernaut. It slowed, all doors opening at once.

Carter led them to one end of an almost deserted car and stood between them and the few passengers. He was the ultimate authority figure, a man to avoid.

They rode past five stations, each announced before arrival from a public-address system. The next station was announced as they pulled away. It was all too simple. No one bothered them. Even the night guard who patrolled after ten o'clock recognized the dreaded uniforms and gave them wide berth.

As the group marched up the steps of Belorusskaya Station, Frannie Miner signaled to Carter with a slight nod of her head and he followed her around a corner to Voevodina Street and a large covered van. The street was deserted, well chosen, free from residential occupancy and prying eyes.

Alice Hodgson handed each child into the truck with a word of encouragement and a pat on the back. When she turned to him, her eyes were moist. No words were necessary as the truck pulled away.

Carter walked beside Alice to the car they had left in a side street. She drove in silence to their apartment and slipped up the back stairs, making no noise.

Without warning, she turned to him, her body shaking,

crying for the children who still had to undergo an ordeal before they were safely home.

He held her. She clung to him. He flicked on a light and she flinched in his arms.

"No. Turn off the light, please."

He flipped off the light and led her to the bed. He tried to untangle her arms and stretch her out, to let her sleep it off, but she continued to cling to him.

"Don't let me go. I need you with me," she said as she slipped a hand beneath his coat and inside his shirt.

Slowly he withdrew her hand and pulled the coat from her. She did the same for him and continued the process, taking off his tie and peeling the shirt from his back. When he was naked to the waist, she pressed her head to his chest, an ear hot against his skin.

It was as if the rescue had brought out a feeling of deep hurt, a reminder of the cruel process of oppression she had fought against for years at almost impossible odds—and she had just saved a score of defenseless innocents from the same fate.

He rocked with her until she whispered something he didn't catch. She started to tug at his belt and pull at his pants and repeated the demand. "I need you, Nick. Please. I need to be close to you."

He undressed her as she tried to hold on to him, then lay with her on top of the bed, her hands never leaving him as if he were her life preserver in a cruel and violent sea.

She was beautiful. Her body, which he'd seen nude before, but never with these emotions, was perfect, from the full and proud breasts to the rounded tummy, from her long, athletic legs to her smoothly curved bottom. And her skin was hot, as if she were in torment.

She melted her mouth against his and pressed herself

to him. He'd thought she needed someone to hang on to, to lie with in silent reassurance, but it was more than that. She needed release. She needed to feel that she was loved, desirable, worthy. She didn't have to tell him how she felt in words; her body was talking for her. Her mouth was aflame. As she crossed a leg over his, he felt the heat of her loins and the moisture that passion had churned from the depths of her.

Their joining seemed as natural as breathing. She cried out as he entered her, then sighed, her hot breath against the side of his neck.

Excitement built up in him like a raging forest fire. This was a rare gift, seldom given. It was the trust of a wounded animal for the one person it trusted to take the hurt away.

She made the act a thing of great joy—from the heat of her, to the fresh youth of her body, to the total commitment, to the opening up and giving of self in complete trust.

He was about to peak early, something he tried to avoid when his special sense of danger warned him that they were not alone. Passion waned as he started to turn, but it was too late. Something crashed against the side of his head. He spasmed and pulled from her as she screamed. Then all was dark and still.

# TEN

The first thing Carter felt as his senses reported back to work was one hell of a headache that was not confined to the place where he had been hit. The first thing outside himself that attracted conscious thought was a low voice, a persuasive voice, speaking in Russian.

*"And the man you work with is Nick Carter."*

*"Yes. Nick Carter."*

*"Where have they taken the children, comrade?"*

*"I am not your comrade."*

Carter's eyes opened to slits. A woman was sitting beside the nude body of Alice Hodgson at the bedside. She held a needle in her hand, about to extract it from her victim's arm. His mind was cast back to Serbsky and the horrible mind-destroying drugs he'd seen white-coated men use there.

*"But you are, comrade. You can never escape our training. You will be back in the program in days—if you survive this,"* the woman said.

The woman was familiar. Sue Setzel. Crisp had in-

troduced them and they were going to work together on
the rest of the assignment. Sue Setzel was using a drug
to interrogate Alice. She'd spoken in Russian. She'd
called Alice her comrade. Shit! They'd turned her. Or
she'd been a double agent from the beginning. Damn
that fool Crisp, that pompous incompetent ass!

Carter tested the ropes at his wrists and found she'd
done a professional job on the knots. But others had done
the same and he'd been able to free himself. He willed
himself to forget the two women for the moment. His
mind took over and he went back to the days long ago
spent with Indian gurus. He'd learned three forms of
yoga to train his mind, body, and inner self. Control of
the muscles had been part of it.

*"Tell me where they are going to take the children,"*
the relentless voice went on.

He didn't hear them.

*"To a place in Estonia. I don't remember."*

*"It doesn't matter. Estonia is enough. We can over-
take them and bring them back."*

As Carter returned to an awareness of his surroundings
the two women were the center of his attention. But
something was terribly wrong. Alice's eyes rolled up in
her head. Sweat broke out all over her body. She con-
vulsed once . . . a terrible shudder than ran through the
beautiful length of her . . . then she was still.

The woman, whoever she really was, slapped Alice
on the face, left and right, but she got no response. She
put her ear to the young woman's chest and cursed softly
in Russian.

Carter bellowed out his rage. Alice had become another victim of Serbsky's infamy. She'd followed thousands who'd been killed by Soviet truth drugs
administered by amateurs. It enraged him.

"So you're awake, Carter." The woman walked to stand in front of him just as his left wrist slipped free. "I shall be doubly honored," she went on, her face twisted in a mocking smile. "I shall bring the children back and turn over the notorious Killmaster at the same time."

Both hands free but kept hidden, he stared at her with eyes filled with hate. "So you fooled Crisp. Very clever. Just who are you?"

"No harm for you to know now, Nick Carter, the great Killmaster, helpless, tied to a chair. The great man's career is finally at an end, and he wants to know my name. I am flattered," she scoffed. "I am Eva Norcross. Strange name for a Soviet agent is it not? I was married to a general in East Germany. Poor fellow had a weak heart."

Carter could not control himself. From a calculating agent, the best, a killing machine that worked only as needed and on the highest of targets, something snapped in the well-ordered brain, and his hands flew out, going for her throat.

The look of surprise never left her face as he used a maniacal strength to squeeze and twist her neck almost all the way around. The bone snapped like a rifle shot.

He freed his legs and went to Alice. She was past hope, her brain fried by the drug, no longer able to control her body. He covered her and wept a silent tear for her. She was worth more than this.

But he had work to do. He dressed as Philip Rolfe, picked up his radio-cassette player, and tuned it to the satellite used by AXE's computer.

"Give me Howard," he said, brushing off the electronic voice's usual syrupy greeting.

"Bad business, Howard. Listen to this carefully. I can

only broadcast a few seconds," he said, holding the microphone close and whispering into the machine. "Alice is dead. Sue Setzel was a double agent; her real name was Eva Norcross. I've terminated her. Both bodies are at the apartment Crisp provided."

He lit a cigarette with hands that were shaking from the cold, and perhaps from the shock. "Tell Lynch that Crisp is an incompetent. Send a cleanup crew to this apartment," he said, giving the address. "I'll be in the boiler room of the Moscow Hotel with friends."

He gave Schmidt a code that told the man in Washington that the Killmaster would call back in an hour to avoid someone triangulating on the signal.

He waited the hour and called in again.

"I need a strong knockout drug that can pollute a whole water supply—powder form—delivered to the hotel boiler room. Tell the CJCS to have three B-2 Stealth bombers standing by at Eielson. Strip them down for human cargo, as many as fifteen to a plane. That's about two thousand pounds of cargo. Put a half-dozen marines on each plane. Got that?"

"Anything else?"

"What about the cluster bomb adaptation we talked about?"

"Completed."

"Try to figure out how to apply it. Can't come in with the C-32 transports. The Tomcats from the carrier can't handle it or the F-16s. Maybe a helicopter. Okay?"

"Over and out."

Carter didn't trust himself to go back to the embassy. If he did, he'd have a hell of a time keeping himself from Crisp's throat. He crammed all the equipment he'd need into the Yugo and drove to the hotel. The boiler room would have to be his home until he headed north to the Spetsnaz camp. He'd taken a last look at the cold body of Alice Hodgson and the distorted face of the enemy. They were a contrast in good and evil. And he didn't ever want to forget the difference.

Ten of the dissidents were in the boiler room when he made his entrance. He'd brought everything from the car.

"You will be bringing the woman with you?" the giant engineer asked.

He told them about the two deaths. They were silent for a while and then shook off the shock. They came to life, more anxious than ever to strike a blow for freedom.

"I have been to Pestovo since I last saw you," a small man at the front of the group announced. "I am called Rudolph Moltsev."

"How did you travel, Rudolph?" Carter asked.

"I have the truck of a collective farm. It is old but inconspicuous."

"You have told your people at Pestovo what we will be doing?"

"I have."

"We will not leave until your friend Frances Miner returns. Tomorrow I will need a messenger to take the car I've been using back to the American embassy. The same man, or woman, will pick up a parcel for me."

"That will be my job," the man from the Metro announced. "I have a Class One travel pass."

"Then it is settled. Frannie should be back in a few hours. We will start after I receive my parcel tomorrow."

The ride between Moscow and Pestovo was about three hundred miles. Two hundred as the crow flies, but the route was far from the best highways. They had to travel

back roads, northeast to Dubna and Kimry, east to Tor-
zhok, northeast again to Bezhetsk, then north to
Yes'vegonsk.

Weary from the long ride, Frannie and Moltsev led
Carter to an old deserted barn. It had been part of a
collective farm but the land in the neighborhood had been
eroded by rains and misuse. It had been taken over for
military purposes. An air base was in the last stage of
construction outside the old town and the junior ranks of
the military could be seen on the streets at all hours.
They were about ten miles from Pestovo and that suited
Carter's purpose perfectly.

Inside the barn Carter was treated to a surprise. Instead
of rotting hay and decaying stalls, the place had been
fitted out as a meeting house with several small sleeping
rooms at the back. They assigned one to him.

"What is the first thing we will do?" Moltsev asked,
his eyes bright, his whole attitude positive.

"I'm going to have a long night's sleep. It might be
my last for a long time," Carter announced. "While I'm
resting I want you to do a few things for me."

"Anything, Comrade Carter. Whatever you need,"
the small man said, eager to get on with it.

"Don't be so obvious, friend Moltsev," Carter
warned. "Calm down. We have time. We must do this
right. And above all, we must not look out of place—
or *you* should not look out of place."


Carter slept through the night, more than ten hours.
He awoke refreshed and feeling as strong as he'd felt
before the stabbing in Washington. Frannie had a breakfast of sausage and hot cereal prepared for him, and some
strong black coffee. When they had finished, the people
of Yes'vegonsk started to drift in, a few at a time.

Carter joined them in the large room. It was obvious that they knew who he was. In this case, he didn't mind. His life was going to be in their hands and a little hero worship wouldn't hurt.

He carried a large bundle to the center table and started to open it. They all gathered around. He uncovered the bright new uniform of a KGB colonel and one of a captain. Those around him caught their breath as he donned the uniform and Frannie followed suit. To them, the uniforms meant trouble, often death.

"Today I will visit the installation at Pestovo. Captain Miner will accompany me as my driver. Did you get the car?"

"The car is outside," one of the men said proudly.

They all trooped out to look at the shining black Zil, the property of a local commissar who was in Moscow for a few days. Carter handed them fender flags from his bundle of goodies and they were mounted in seconds. The car looked very official, particularly in the rural setting.

Inside, he stood behind the table, an impressive figure, while they squatted around him.

"Are the cooks here?" he asked.

A few hands were raised, the faces conveying mixed emotions, proud to serve but not knowing what was expected of them.

Carter took two small sacks from his bundle and placed them before him. "One for the base at Pestovo. One for the new air base," he announced.

A man came to take one sack. He announced he was the principal cook at Pestovo. A woman took the other. She was from the air base.

"You will put this chemical in the water supply tonight while everyone sleeps. It is slow acting. By tomorrow night everyone on each base will be under the control of a nerve drug that will paralyze them for more than twenty-four hours,'' Carter announced. ''You will not be killing anyone. Is that clear?''

They all nodded.

''It is imperative that every person on each base be out of action. But we have several problems still,'' Carter said.

''What are they?'' Moltsev said, obviously a leader of the group.

''Someone must operate the telephone system and the radio communications. We must offer false security to anyone who calls. The idea will be to delay for as long as possible,'' Carter continued in Russian.

''That will be my job,'' a woman at the back spoke up. ''It will be taken care of.''

''We need someone to control the new landing strip lights,'' Carter added.

''How will it be done, Comrade Carter?'' Moltsev asked.

''I will give you the hour. Someone must flash the lights on and off twice. That's all. Any more will be noted, perhaps by spy satellite.''

''Why the lights?'' the little man asked, his mind obviously working overtime. Good. They needed people like him.

''The planes that are coming have computers that will plot a landing from the two brief flashes.''

''What else is needed?'' a pale woman from the back asked.

''We may have to transport as many as fifty children to the planes from Pestovo. We will need people to go in, carry out the bodies, and transport them to the planes. It must be done quickly. We don't want the planes on the ground for more than a few minutes."

"That will be my job," one of the men said. He was a brute of a man, bull-like, but his voice was soft as down. "I am the master mechanic for the camp at Pestovo. I control the trucks."

"And I can get two dozen people to carry bodies," another called out.

"I am trusting Comrade Moltsev to coordinate all of this. Make sure everyone involved has a fresh supply of water tonight. No one will drink water or eat food containing our chemical after the water supply is contaminated," Carter warned. "Starting at midnight tonight, you will use your own supply."

They all nodded.

"Captain Miner and I will visit the camp tomorrow. We will not eat or drink there. We will return here and meet with you all at eighteen hundred hours, that's six o'clock. If any of you can't make it, I might not see you again. I want to thank you on behalf of the children."

One of the men, probably the oldest one there, stood on wobbly knees and spoke with emotion. "We have known of this abomination for a long time, comrade. It is a national disgrace," he said, wiping a tear from his eye. "But you understand we could do nothing about it. We are simple peasants." He was barely able to carry on. They all waited, respecting the old man. "It is we who thank you. I will carry out at least one child on these old legs and I will be proud."

When they had gone, leaving Carter and Frannie alone, he stripped off his tie and sat back in an overstuffed chair, lighting a cigarette. "Do they think of the future?" he asked.

"And what does that mean?"

"Reprisals. The Soviets are not stupid. They'll know

we could not pull it off ourselves. Some will go to the gulags.''

"Don't sell them short, Nick. They've been survivors from the day they were born.''

# ELEVEN

Carter sat behind Frannie in the Zil as they pulled up
to the guardhouse at Pestovo.

"Identification," the sergeant of the guard snapped
out. The contingent of five men all had Kalashnikov
automatic rifles slung over their shoulders. But the AK-
47s were only a small part of their armament. They
carried three hundred rounds and fifty grenades for their
special commando model AKs. Each rifle was equipped
with a dull metal bayonet that doubled as a saw and a
wire cutter. Each man carried a P6 silenced pistol and
another knife that was spring-loaded. It could shoot a
blade accurately up to thirty feet. They were dressed in
camouflaged battle gear, complete with full body armor.
Their eyes were cold and they never let them roam from
the shining car.

"Your car is very clean after so long a drive, Colonel," the sergeant said. The dreaded uniform of the KGB
colonel seemed to hold no fear for him. This was a man
who knew his job.

"I stayed with an old acquaintance at Rybinsk. His people were attentive," Carter said, his tone cold. "I commend you on your powers of observation, Sergeant. But I question your targets. Don't *ever* try that old trick on me again."

"Yes, sir!" the sergeant snapped out, handing back the identification Schmidt had provided. He saluted and waved at the men to open the gate.

"I almost pissed my pants," Frannie said, turning her head. "Did you see those animals? Howard made me read up on them, but at the time I thought it sounded like something out of science fiction."

"They're real enough. And the place is probably crawling with them."

"No wonder you wanted them all asleep. This place would be impregnable."

"Now you're beginning to understand. Just stay cool. Remember, all of these people breakfasted here this morning. The drug is already working on them."

"Something bothers me about the drug. If they don't all crash at once, someone's going to get to the outside and call for help."

"I thought of that, smartie. While you were sleeping, I talked to Moltsev. His people have already taken over all communications. I helped them."

"You took out some of these apes? You replaced them with our people?"

"It was necessary."

She shook her head slowly. "Boy, I'd sure like to get this one over with. How long do you think it will take?"

"I don't know. I'm not sure it was the right plan. But we're into it now, so we play it out."

"Why did you choose these uniforms?" she asked.

"You forget your training. I'll have to remind Howard

to work on you," he teased. They had only a minute before meeting the camp commandant. Carter was feeling a little tense and knew Frannie's gut had to be in knots. "We are Department Five, the Executive Action Branch. It's like Himmler's SS when Hitler came to power. Even the colonel here—he's with the First Chief Directorate, First Department—he should shit himself when he learns that he's under our scrutiny."

"What has he got to fear?"

"That's the point. He doesn't know and he'll be worried about it until the drug takes over."

"Why are we still using the names you and Alice used in Moscow?"

"Because Howard goofed for the first time in living memory. Our identity cards show the same names both times. Maybe he thought we'd get confused if we had to remember new names every time we turned around."

"Do I look like an Ivan?" she asked nervously.

"Just pray that they don't notice, Captain Sokol."

They pulled up at the administration building and were ushered into the colonel's office with no delay.

"Colonel Marchenko," the colonel's aide, a young captain, saluted when he'd glanced at Carter's card. "A pleasure, sir."

It was anything but a pleasure. The captain had broken out in a sweat and was obviously nervous as he announced them.

"Colonel Marchenko of Department Five, Commandant Krotkov," the young man said, beating a quick retreat to his own office.

The commandant of Pestovo was a rugged specimen, as Carter had expected. This was a prize posting. He was in his mid-thirties and fit as a heavyweight the day before a championship fight. He held out a hand. His smile was forced. "I was not expecting you, comrade."

"No one ever does. But your case is different," Carter
said, taking off his greatcoat and hat. He put them on
an empty chair and sat in front of the colonel's desk
without being asked. Frannie sat in a chair in the corner
of the room.

Krotkov looked them over and slowly sat behind his
desk. The smile faded. "How different?" he asked.

"Because I've been sent here for two reasons. I have
to look over your operation. You know that. But I'm
also here to commend you. My department head is impressed with what he sees on paper. "

"I am pleased," Krotkov said, but he didn't appear
to accept the facts readily.

"I also have a confession to make," Carter said. "I
wanted to see your recruits in action."

The smile was genuine this time. "I have to turn away
many curious officers, Colonel. If you didn't have other
official business . . . well . . . you don't show this operation to just anyone." He reached for a coffee mug beside
him that was almost full and obviously still warm.

"Will you have some coffee, Colonel?" he asked.

"No. But the drive was cold. You know how it is,"
Carter said.

"Of course," the big man said, pouring vodka into
two small glasses. He pushed one over to Carter and
carried the other to Frannie.

"I've never had a man of your rank visit me with a
junior officer in tow, Colonel. And I've been asking
myself why that is."

"Habit, Colonel. Captain Sokol is an unimpeachable
witness and she has a photographic memory. Both traits
are invaluable in my business."

"Unimpeachable? I don't understand."

"The daughter of a general, granddaughter to a former First Minister. Very useful, Colonel."

Krotkov blanched as much as it was possible for the man. He kept his eyes from contact with Frannie's as if the glance would give him an incurable disease. "Would you like a tour?" he asked.

Carter finished his vodka and rose, reaching for his greatcoat. "I'd be delighted. I should really be heading back in an hour."

"You can't stay for lunch, comrade?" Krotkov asked, warming somewhat.

*And a chance to digest some of my own powder?* Carter thought. "No. But we thank you. This has got to be a fast visit."

They went out into the crunch of fresh snow underfoot. It had started to fall after they entered the building and was coming down as fine powder. It gave the camp an antiseptic appearance.

"The barracks will be empty," Krotkov said, "but we'll take a swing through them regardless. As you know, you can tell a great deal about the camp from an empty barracks room.

"This is for the boys," the commandant said as they entered a Quonset-hut-like structure.

It was long and narrow. Carter's agile mind catalogued double bunks on either side, thirty-six occupied, fourteen not. The symmetry was the first thing he noticed after counting. Each bunk was placed to create a perfect pattern of perspective as they stood at the door looking at the long, symmetrical row. Each bed was made perfectly, none with the hint of a crease. The barracks boxes at the foot of each bed shone as if varnished several times. A spare pair of boots rested on either side of the barracks box, every one spotless, gleaming in the midmorning light.

Krotkov opened one box and revealed snow-white underwear pressed and folded on one side, heavy gray socks on the other. He lifted the socks to reveal clean shirts and sleeping apparel underneath.

He opened a second box. It was the same as the first— exactly.

"Impressive," Carter said. "How long do they stay with you?"

"Two years."

"By comparison, how long do we give our *Spetsnaya Naznacheniya*?"

"You have not taken the training, Colonel?" Krotkov asked, his lip curled with scorn. "Surely with more than thirty thousand trained, I was sure you would have been one."

"We will not all be privileged to be at the forefront, Colonel. How long?"

"Three months."

"So we give these spineless children eight times as much training?"

"You don't understand the philosophy, Colonel. They have a natural resistance. Our Spetsnaz recruits are mostly the best men in their unit when we get them."

"But the decadent young women cannot keep up. Is that not right?" Carter asked, prodding the man in the direction he wanted him to go.

"You will see them in action, Colonel."

"I'd like to see their barracks block first."

Krotkov frowned at the man beside him. He stopped in his tracks. "Why?" he asked suspiciously.

"You said it yourself. You can tell a great deal from its appearance."

The big man smiled. He was relishing the victory. He marched them to the girls' dormitory and flung the door open. "See for yourself."

Carter's eyes flicked once over the long room making a mental picture of it. Forty beds occupied, ten empty. So they had seventy-six victims instead of the fifty he'd expected. This was the main reason for his visit, but that was not all of it. "I'm convinced," Carter said, patting the big colonel on the back lightly. It was a token gesture, but a miraculous catalyst for the Soviet commandant.

"I've heard we teach them to kill here," Carter prodded.

"And you are lucky. Ten of the most difficult recruits will be blooded today."

"Blooded?" Frannie spoke up for the first time. "How could you possibly do that?"

"Your grandfather apparently didn't confide in you, Captain. All our top soldiers will have killed before they go into battle."

"But why is this necessary for these children?" she persisted, her face not revealing the revulsion Carter knew she must be feeling.

"When they are graduated, and that will be years from now, they must be trained to kill without compunction, to follow any order no matter how gruesome."

"Have you ever failed, Colonel?" Carter asked.

"We don't fail. They might fail, but we don't. We have a graveyard filled with the ones who were unsuitable."

Carter thought of the book he'd taken from Lumumba and sent to Washington. The book would be invaluable in unraveling this whole mess after the system was destroyed. He hadn't counted on the cemetery or how it might make him feel while he was forced to keep a neutral expression. It was all he could do to keep from throttling the man beside him now.

Before they reached the blooding grounds, they came across the first sign of trouble. A Spetsnaz had collapsed and two others were taking him to the infirmary.

"What's this?" the colonel demanded.

"Maybe a little food poisoning, Colonel," one of the Spetsnaz said, trying to salute. "Or maybe he just overdid it this time. Sergei eats like a hog."

"Carry on. But report this man's name to my orderly."

Carter and Frannie looked at each other. It was the beginning. Would everyone start dropping like flies now, or would it take a long time? They were as vulnerable as hell and they knew it.

Krotkov apparently forgot the incident and strode with purpose toward a large open area. They could hear men and women shouting and others screaming.

When they turned the corner, the scene was shocking. Two dozen Spetsnaz, fully armed, were in charge of about twenty recruits, mostly young girls from twelve to fourteen.

One of the girls was walking back from a huddled form in the middle of the arena. The mutilated body was immobile, a mass of glistening red flesh. The girl carried a Kalashnikov with a bayonet on the end. The blade and the barrel were covered with blood. Her arms were stained with blood, fresh, still shining, dulled as the light snowfall covered it.

The others were howling like animals. Some had bloody arms; others did not. While they watched in horrified fascination, one of the girls, no more than five feet tall, dressed in the green fatigues of the recruit, took her place at the side of a chute. The setup reminded Carter of a rodeo calf roping that he'd seen once in Colorado.

Suddenly a Spetsnaz shoved a bayonet between the bars of a small cage as another opened the gate. Something came out on the run, a bundle of rags, a man of skin and bone. His rump dripped of blood while his feet, wrapped in rags, churned on the half-frozen mud of the arena.

The girl took after him like a young gazelle. He was no more than fifteen feet from the gate when the bayonet came flashing up in an arc and pierced his skin below his right shoulder blade.

"They are taught never to go for a heart on the first thrust," Krotkov said, his eyes shining with pleasure. "This one was particularly difficult. Last week was her tenth try and she could not do it. But look at her now. She will kill him slowly as she's been taught. Then she will be given the next test and she will pass it.

"This is why we are superior to the decadent American capitalists, Marchenko. This is the steel of the Soviet heart."

While they watched, the youngster felled the prisoner with the butt of her rifle, pinned him to the dust with thrusts to all his extremities while he shrieked out his pain. In a horrible climax, she flipped him on his back, and with his eyes as big as saucers, she sliced through his carotid arteries, then skewered him through the heart, the blood pouring from him like water from a leaky garden hose.

She returned to the pack of howling children triumphant.

"I'm going to be sick," Frannie whispered to him in English.

The use of their language froze him in shock. "If you even come close, I'll club you senseless as my role model would. No way you can disgrace your colonel now," he whispered in Russian.

But the next act was so totally unexpected, Carter was not disturbed by Frannie's reaction. Another prisoner was prodded out and a youth took off after him. He garrotted the skeletonlike captive, then dragged him to a wooden pole Carter hadn't noticed and tied him expertly.

When the captive was helpless, the youth pulled a commando knife from his belt and gutted the helpless man, starting at his breastbone and running the knife left and right as he opened the man to his crotch.

The group of kids went into a frenzy at the sight of the blood and the entrails of the victim slowly spilling to the snow.

Frannie moved to a shed nearby and threw up as promised. Krotkov sneered at the sight and waved Carter back to his office.

As they turned to go, one of the Spetsnaz clutched at his stomach and fell to his knees, followed by another and a third. Two of the blood-soaked children toppled over and lay still.

"What . . . ? What the hell is going on here?" Krotkov barked, heading for his office on the run.

Carter followed, and turned to make sure that Frannie caught up. They burst into the outer office to find the young captain slumped over his desk, his tongue lolling, saliva forming a small puddle beside the blotter on his desk.

Krotkov reached for the telephone. "Give me the infirmary!" he screamed out, his control gone.

"What do you mean, the lines are all busy? *Break in!*"

He listened for a couple of seconds. "Then get me regional headquarters!"

"But *all* lines can't be busy! Hello? *Hello?*"

He slammed down the receiver. "The damned operator must have passed out. What the hell's going on?" he shouted in desperation.

Then his features changed. From a desperate man he looked cunning again. "It's you, isn't it. You show up and my men start dropping."

He reached for his gun and had it out of his holster, when Frannie fired. The bullet missed Carter by inches. She had room to crease the Soviet's arm, not to kill him.

He bellowed like a bull and came at them, a mountain of a man, his training forgotten, his arms reaching out like tree limbs about to enfold them. But when he reached Carter he was caught up short. With a flick of the wrist, Hugo had appeared in Carter's hand, the long, thin blade now piercing the heart of the man who would have killed him.

Time seemed to stand still for a moment as the giant loomed over Carter, a surprised look on his face. He started to clutch at his chest as the blade was removed, then he sunk to his knees, the life gone out of him.

"Get them into Krotkov's office," Carter commanded, grasping the big man by the collar and sliding him through the door, using the mat he'd fallen on as a skid.

Frannie had some trouble with the weight of the captain, but she managed to get him in the office and behind the desk beside the commandant.

Carter was at work pulling the drapes. He searched Krotkov for keys and waved Frannie to the door. "Get to the car!" he commanded, searching the bunch of keys for the right one. When the door was locked, he followed her to the car, picking three P6s from fallen Spetsnaz on the way.

"Let's get back. We've still got a lot of work to do today."

Two hours later, dressed in black commando gear, armed with his own weapons and the three P6s, Carter led the small army of dissidents back to the camp. This time they were not challenged.

They found bodies everywhere. Moltsev was in charge of the trucks. He was to count the bodies retrieved until he had the full seventy-six. He and his men had been warned that some would be blood-splattered, not that the fact mattered much to these courageous souls.

As they advanced, a Spetsnaz warrior spun around a corner but before he could fire, Carter put a slug from a silenced P6 through his heart.

The whole camp looked like a battlefield. The dissidents, men and women, began carrying the kids to the trucks. They piled them up like cordwood. Bruises and scrapes were the least of their worries.

Frannie, dressed like Carter, and fully trained as a commando, was responsible to retrieve her people who had been at the communications shacks.

Carter placed himself close to the trucks that had been driven in the gates and turned to face outward before loading. Other Spetsnaz, less affected by the chemical, made an effort to get at their civilian invaders, but Carter's aim was true. The Killmaster was quick, but not quick enough to catch them all. One dissident, carrying one of the kids, was sprayed with 7.62mm slugs, catching one in each shoulder. The youngster on his shoulder was shot in the groin. Dissidents assigned to first-aid duty tended to them.

"One of our people in the radio room has been shot," Frannie shouted as she escorted two of the heroes who had managed the telephone exchange back to the trucks.

Carter took off at a trot. On the way a Spetsnaz kicked up dirt all around him, emptying his orange plastic AK magazine at the man from AXE, slicing a piece of leather from one boot and creasing a toe. Carter fired on the run and saw the man go down.

The radio room was a shambles. One of his people was beyond help; the other was hit in three places but still breathing. Carter picked up the live one and, with blood dripping from his wounded toe, ran back to the truck, his P6 picking off targets as he ran.

He turned the wounded man over to the medics and was about to leave. "Where are you going?" Frannie asked. "We've got more than sixty kids on board."

"The dead man at the telephone exchange. We're not leaving any of our dead behind. And I want one of the commandant's aides. They might like to interrogate him back home."

Frannie shouted an order for someone to pick up the drugged young captain. Then she picked up an AK-47 and a couple of clips from a fallen Spetsnaz. She arrived at the shack as Carter was picking up the dead man. A Spetsnaz, wracked with pain, his rifle pointed at Carter, was about to spray the room. She almost cut him in half as ten 7.62s traced a line across his gut.

The exit was as fast as they could make it. They'd been in the camp for no more than five minutes. The road back was almost deserted. While they bumped from rut to rut, Carter radioed the coordinates for the airport to the AXE computer with instructions for the cruising B-2s to come in now. He checked his watch. In the last few minutes, the ground team would have flashed the runway lights and the whole topographical area would be recorded on the B-2s' electronic navigation imager.

Timing was critical. The B-2 bombers, each worth billions, could only be on the ground for minutes.

At the airport, Carter made a quick hard probe. He found one Spetsnaz, almost out but not quite unconscious. Before the enemy soldier could bring his rifle to bear, to dredge up all his strength to overcome the drug, one shot from a silenced P6 stopped him—permanently. The P6s had been a lucky find. Wilhelmina was still Carter's number one lady, but the silenced Soviet guns gave him an edge.

The trucks lined up on the side of the runway. Faces filled with wonder watched in awe as the three huge gull-winged birds came in at low altitude and settled on the cement runway without so much as a shudder. The huge V-shaped black planes taxied back to the beginning of the runway, turned into the wind, and waited for the loading.

Carter talked to the crew leader while scores of Frannie's people loaded their prizes into the small holds of the aircraft.

"A dude name of Schmidt gave us a package for you," the captain said. "Big sucker, lots of gray hair, weird-looking gent."

"Thanks. You have any trouble on the way in?"

"None. If we loose these babies, Uncle Sammy's going to be one mad son of a bitch."

"The President and the CJCS think that rescuing more than seventy of our kids is worth it. Now get the hell out of here," Carter said. "And thanks."

The Stealth bomber pilots, working close to two major Soviet cities, had flown in with impunity and the odds were they'd do the same on their way out. The planes' design, the texture of their outer skin, and the electronic jamming gear on board made detection impossible.

When the jet-black birds had lifted off and the seventy-six American kids were on their way back home, the dissidents all crowded around Carter, their faces wreathed in smiles. "What's next?" Frannie asked, as eager as the others to finish the job.

Carter waved his hands to silence them. "You've all been great. We owe you a great deal and we won't forget. But I've got to do the next step by myself."

A groan from dozens of throats was his answer. These were good people, Soviets to the core, but not motivated by twisted ideals of world domination. They were like most of the people here, satisfied if they had the essentials of life, unaccustomed to finery, and content to be allowed enough freedom to shed the pall of fear that was a curtain over them. The last thoughts they harbored was conquering anything beyond a reasonable lifestyle.

"I need help from someone with aircraft experience," Carter told them.

"I'm a mechanic," one of the women at the back of the crowd said waving a hand.

Carter moved to her and took her to one side as the crowd disbursed. "I've got a very long way to go and I'd like to get there as fast as possible," he told her.

"Are you a pilot?" she asked.

"I'm not the best, but I can handle most light planes."

"I didn't have a light one in mind, comrade. I work on an old Ilyushin IL14. It's not pressurized, has a range of only twelve hundred and fifty miles, but I can change that. Where are you going?"

"Middle of the Chukchi Peninsula. Almost three thousand miles."

"This bird could be fixed up to fly that far. If I had enough time, you could have auxiliary tanks welded inside. It would be risky."

"No problem. How much time do you need?"

"How much have I got?"

"Maybe two hours."

"Then I'll get help and do it in less than two hours."

"How fast is this bird?"

"Slow, comrade—two-forty or two-fifty at best. You'll be in the air for twelve to fourteen hours."

"You've got maps?"

"I'll get them for you."

Carter thought about the problems. Lots of problems. What else did he need to know? "How would you do it, comrade?" he asked.

"I'm not crazy enough, but you might make it. Without the usual forty-eight-hundred-pound payload—we'd replace that with gasoline—you'll be a flying gas tank. You'll have to fly at treetop level to avoid radar. You'll have to stay awake one hell of a long time, and when you get there, you'll have to parachute out far enough from the camp to avoid detection when the crate plows into a mountain. Better you than me, comrade."

Carter smiled to himself at the speech. He could get to like this woman. "Will you ask someone to put my packages in a container and have it attached to a parachute?"

"What's in it?"

"Explosives."

She looked at him and her broad face broke into a crinkly grin "Mad," she said. "You're a madman."

"Can you handle it, comrade?" he asked. "I'm going to get some sleep."

"I can do it."

"Wake me when you're finished."

He turned to look for Frannie and found her talking to a half dozen of her friends. "Better get them out of here," he advised. "These animals should be awake in a few hours and you'd be better off miles from here."

"I heard you talking to Magda. I could spell you at the controls, act as your adjutant when you get there."

"I'm going in alone, Frannie. It looks like a one-man job."

"I could keep you warm on cold nights."

"All the nights are cold where I'm going."

"Sounds better all the time."

He held out his arms to her and she came into them. They held each other for almost a minute, then she turned to her charges and herded them into the trucks. "I'm leaving a driver for Magda. Make sure she's out of here when you leave."

The office at the *Glavnoye Razvedyatelnoye Upravleniye* headquarters in Moscow was a beehive. Everyone seemed to be walking on eggs. General Ryabov, head of the GRU, the Soviet counterpart of American G2 military intelligence, sat at his desk, his face chalk white. Three colonels stood at attention in front of the desk. Their faces registered the shock that the bad news had engendered.

"Does the First Minister know?" Ryabov asked.

"Not to our knowledge, sir," one of the colonels snapped out.

"Oh, sit the hell down," he said wearily. "Is this really as bad as it looks?"

"Sir, when our most efficient Spetsnaz camp is rendered useless and all of the recruits kidnapped, it can't get any worse."

They sat for a moment, each with his own thoughts.

"How do you suppose they did it?" Ryabov asked, his whole demeanor changed, his appearance that of a

defeated man. Just hours ago, he'd been one of the most
powerful and feared men in the Soviet Union. His mind
was in a turmoil. He'd seen other men go down in flames,
their careers ruined by one major blunder. But nothing
could compare with this. The project was the First Minister's proudest accomplishment. Even though he'd stolen the idea from Ruzimatov, he'd been swept into power
on the strength of the successful project, the most daring
and innovative in the history of international intelligence.
Nothing before or since had come close to the magnitude
of its value to their cause.

How in hell could he face Yevgeny Popolov? They
had been boyhood friends and the friendship had blos-
somed through the years. They had neighboring dachas
on the Black Sea. Their wives were like sisters. But all
of that meant nothing compared to the magnitude of his
failure. And it was all so unfair. How could he have
prevented it?

His massive frame was shaken by an equally massive
sigh. The colonels remained silent while he brooded.

"We'll have to warn Kivak," he finally said. "I received word that the Lumumba complex was raided too
late to strengthen Pestovo sufficiently, but we can't lose
Kivak as well."

"But you could have done nothing, General," one of
the colonels offered. "Someone used a drug in the water
supply at Pestovo and the airstrip. No one could with-
stand that."

"Then tell me how they got them out. How do they
carry away more than seventy teen-agers? The recruits
would be like human land mines to handle, a sack full
of deadly snakes. I'm not even sure they can be repro-
grammed. So how could they take them to a port and
get them out? Tell me. You're supposed to be my best

men. *How the hell did it happen?"* he asked, pounding on his desk.

They all sat ramrod straight. They were in this as deep as he and they were all terrified that they had reached the end of the road, a road that had been paved with gold until hours ago.

"I'm told they have perfected a bomber undetectable by radar," one of them said tentatively. "Could they . . . ?"

"Don't be a fool!" Ryabov bellowed. "If they could fly in here, load, and take off, then no place in the Soviet Union is safe from them."

"My point exactly," the man persisted.

"Get out of here," he shouted, his jowls flapping with the effort. "One of you inform Kivak and then call the First Minister's aide. And don't disturb me for any reason."

When they had gone, he rose and moved ponderously to the door. He locked it, returned to his swaybacked swivel chair, and punished it with his weight. He pulled a bottle of vodka from his desk, put it to his mouth, and let the fiery liquid spill down his throat until the bottle was empty.

He sat and felt the liquid numb his brain, lessen the mental pain, but open up the floodgates of regret. No one knew better than he the kind of society he had helped create. The rules allowed him to climb over mutilated bodies to the top of the heap, but such rules had their weaknesses. They could permit disaster to change your life with the snap of a finger. The top men at Chernobyl had met the same fate. They were not tried and found wanting. Soviet funds were not available for protracted trials. The wheels of justice were square, useless, almost nonexistent. He had helped invent the rules and they would bring him down.

So that was it for him. He was a dead man. They would come for him. Popolev would take his pound of flesh in the form of a tongue-lashing, then it would be reported that he died mysteriously of some as yet incurable ailment. An incurable ailment, he groaned to himself. An assassin's bullet in the back of the head was always an incurable ailment.

But it would not happen to him. What was a few hours? his besotted brain asked.

His right hand reached into a desk drawer, fumbled awkwardly for an old Makarov, a weapon he'd carried through many campaigns. He checked the load, chambered a round, put the barrel in his mouth, and in one movement, his thoughts channeled in one direction, squeezed the trigger.

# TWELVE

The Union of Soviet Socialist Republics is a huge landmass. The route Carter had to take, as straight as possible, carried him over every kind of geological feature. The land was ribbed across with mountain ranges, some just two or three thousand feet high, others that seemed to stretch to the sky. The Soviets were not plagued by water shortages. It seemed that the ancient craft took him over countless rivers and lakes, the sun's reflection almost blinding at times, as he tried to keep the old bird at the lowest possible altitude.

The task was monumental. His mechanic friend had assured him that the old Ilyushin's motors were in great condition and that had been the truth. What she had failed to mention was what age and use can do to an aircraft.

The control bar had a half inch of play, so that every adjustment in flight was warped by the loose action. It was as if you were in a high-speed chase in an old car and you had to turn the steering wheel an inch or two to get any reaction. Since he had to keep to treetop level, he couldn't put her on autopilot or even hold the control between his knees while he poured a small shot from the bottle of scotch Howard Schmidt had provided as part of the survival gear, or even search for a morsel of food in the pack. Every second had to be devoted to keeping the plane on course. Even the ailerons had the same worn-out characteristic. Carter's ankles were cramped by the constant adjustment of ailerons left or right. Last, the trim tabs, used to fine tune the load and the controls, were almost impossible to set properly because the tanks installed hurriedly in the middle of the cargo hold gave the crate an unusual center of gravity. He felt that he was riding an out-of-control roller coaster with his hands tied behind his back.

The hours dragged on. Carter couldn't believe that he hadn't been spotted. Some of the peasants or officials who saw the plane flash past would call the information to the local military. It was impossible that search planes hadn't been dispatched. But after eight or nine hours in the air, he hadn't been challenged.

He was a little more than halfway to his destination and his normally boundless energy was at a low ebb. In a desperate move, he took her up to five thousand feet, high over the mountains of Popigay, well above the tree line. He put her on autopilot, unpacked a box of hard biscuits from his pack, and took a long pull on the scotch.

Radar operators from Moscow to the Bering Sea had been warned to keep their eyes on their sets every second. Lumumba had been raided and Pestovo had been decimated. All recruits from these camps had been spirited out of the country and officialdom didn't know how. Kivak was obviously the next target. An Ilyushin had been stolen from Pestovo, but it had a range of only 1200 to 1400 miles.

"Alert all air bases between here and Kivak," the base commander at Pestovo screamed at his aides. He felt as if he'd been run over by a truck since reviving from the effects of the drug. He'd been called a dozen times by his superiors in Moscow. Everyone was going crazy. "No Ilyushin will be refueled for any reason," he told them. "Unless the captain has a special pass from the Kremlin, no aircraft in our northern regions will be fueled at all."

"The stolen aircraft has been seen twice over small villages," an aide offered. "Local commissars have reported in. Once, over Popigay, we picked him up on local radar but only for a few seconds."

"How did he get that far without refueling?" the commander screamed, an element of hysteria creeping into his voice.

"We are questioning all local aircraft maintenance people now, sir."

"Forget it. You're going to find at least one missing. What model was the aircraft? What is its capacity?"

"Ilyushin IL14. It's not pressurized, has a range of only twelve hundred and fifty miles, carries only fifteen passengers."

"But we found most of the seats removed," a lowly sergeant offered.

"You're an aircraft mechanic. What does that suggest, Sergeant?"

"Two things are possible, sir. They could have wanted to load more men, as many as thirty. Or they could have pulled the seats out for extra fuel tanks."

"I think . . . Make an inventory of the gasoline storage area immediately. The bastard could have enough gas in

auxiliary tanks to fly to Alaska,'' the commandant said
thoughtfully. ''But it makes more sense that he's on his
way to Kivak.''

''Why do you refer to the enemy as 'he,' sir?'' one
of the junior officers asked.

The commandant was silent for a moment. ''I don't
know, Lieutenant. If the plane is loaded with extra tanks,
it'll have no room for passengers. And I have a feeling
about this. I think Pestovo was hit by one man with the
help of our own people.''

''Our own people?''

''Malcontents, dissidents, nogoodnicks,'' the commandant said, as if to himself. ''The kind of disloyal
groups we see springing up under *glasnost*.'' He sat for
a long time, thinking, his feet on his desk, his hands
behind his head. ''One man. What the hell does he think
he can do at Kivak?''

The pain in his back and arms was almost unbearable.
The load of gas from the interior tanks was gone, so the
aircraft trim was back to normal. He finally knew how
much gas he had left. The wing tanks would take him
another three hundred miles and if his navigation maps
were accurate, he was over Baranhika, five hundred miles
from his target. Shit.

He hadn't seen any enemy aircraft and that seemed
like some kind of miracle. Once or twice he'd seen a
glint of sunlight off something above him, but they hadn't
seen him. It seemed impossible that with all the electronic
gear on the new Soviet fighters they hadn't spotted him
on radar or picked up the heat trail he was leaving behind
him like a meteorite. Maybe it was the shelter of the
mountains that saved him. He'd been weaving in and out

of mountain ranges for hours, the peaks towering over him.

Okay. Time for final preparation. He took her up to ten thousand feet, making himself extremely vulnerable, and moved into the body of the craft to pack for the final descent.

The female mechanic had provided what he needed. All of the goodies that Schmidt sent with the B-2s were in two huge duffel bags and secured to a cargo parachute. He pulled his arms through his parachute, secured the clamps, and returned to the pilot's seat.

Not long to go now. He was down to less than a quarter tank, the reserve tank, about enough for a hundred miles. He made a quick calculation. Three hundred miles to go. One hell of a long way in the arctic tundra. His life was going to be in Schmidt's hands once he hit the ground.

The port engine coughed once and began to stutter.

He turned to port, toward the Chuckchi Sea. He figured he was somewhere close to Rigol. It was time to bail out.

The cargo door was on the starboard side just aft of the wing. It was going to be a bitch to get the cargo out and make his own jump without hitting the tail fins.

He was dressed in a down coat with parka when he pulled the cargo door open, but the arctic air grabbed at him like the cold heart of the Spetsnaz he'd left behind.

Carter followed the cargo out within a split second. Even then it was soon lost in the swirl of snow that was falling in flakes as large as he'd ever seen.

He hit hard and rolled. The snow was not deep, perhaps six inches, but the crust beneath was solid, hard-packed snow, probably many feet thick, and frozen tundra. Carter stood with his legs braced as he slipped out of the parachute. He fought the wind to keep a hold on the chute while he freed himself, then rolled the chute, scooped out a white grave for the cloth, and covered it completely.

He stood in a white world, visibility no more than twenty feet. He took two tentative steps and the tundra collapsed under his weight. He unstrapped a package from his back and assembled a pair of snowshoes of ribbed plastic, no doubt one of the far-out experiments of his imaginative buddy Howard.

But he needed more than that. The wind chill had to be fifty below. He had very little time to find shelter.

Awkwardly, his gloves making the job twice as difficult, he examined his pockets for a solution. In his right-hand jacket pocket he found an unusual battery-operated meter. When he turned it on nothing happened. Slowly he described a circle and the needle of the meter, like a well-trained hunting dog, finally zeroed in on a steady point.

A metal detector. Damned if old Howard wasn't some kind of genius. He started out, awkwardly at first, until he was accustomed to the high leg action of snowshoeing. But the work paid off. A brown mound appeared out of the white blanket. His cargo.

The duffel bags contained a lot of items Carter didn't recognize and some he did. The tent was the first priority. He took it out. It was nylon, triple-layered, strong, and with a complete floor. The pegs were shaped like boat anchors, the only practical thing in arctic tundra.

The heating unit was no more than six inches square and burned a special chemical. When the tent was up and the stove going, Carter stripped off some of his gear and examined the rest of his supplies.

The survival food was compact, light to carry, and plentiful. The stove would make one cup of coffee at a time. He had a lot of electronic components he didn't understand, but that could wait. His tent was secure. His stove would burn for at least four hours without a refill. He curled up in a down sleeping bag and let the white world around him go its own way. He hadn't slept for almost twenty hours. If he was going to attempt the rescue at Kivak, he needed his rest.

Colonel-Doctor Nikolai Leonid Simolin sat in his office, the telephone to his ear. Colonel Igor Victor Sobolev sat across from him, his handsome face creased with a frown that had been present since he'd heard about Lumumba. He was the manager of the underground city of Kivak. It had been conceived ten years earlier when he was a lowly lieutenant. His dreams had been fulfilled. Now the installation was his responsibility. He was still in his thirties, built like a light heavyweight fighter, Spetsnaz trained, and as sharp as most men in command of major installations in the Soviet Union.

But he was still a junior colonel. His boss, Simolin, was in charge of the whole project. Two of the installations had been raided and were virtually out of business. One of the senior officers had taken his life. A plane had been stolen with every indication that it was on its way to Kivak carrying the force that had wiped out the other two camps.

The man on the other end of the line was the new head of the GRU. He'd been appointed by Popolov hours after Ryabov's suicide. They all knew that Ryabov was a crony of Popolov's, but this was war, or about as close to it as you could get.

"I want the man who is heading up this force alive. I want him interrogated. I want the Politburo to see him put to death. We all have to know that nothing like this can ever happen again."

"You can count on us, General."

"That, Nikolai Leonid, is what your friends at Lumumba and Pestovo said. Ryabov was smart to take his own life. Compared to their punishment, his death was simple and uncomplicated," he growled into the telephone, "and we don't want any part of that, do we."

"It will not happen, Comrade General. We are impregnable here."

"One last clue and this is vital. We are sure that the man posed as a colonel on the staff of the Inspector General. Our KGB friends tell us his name is Nick Carter, the best agent the Americans have."

The line was silent for a moment. "He will be alone?" Simolin asked.

"It is his style. Although evidence indicates he had a lot of help at both Lumumba and Pestovo. I can't tell you what to expect."


Carter awoke feeling better than he had for a long time. Even after the ordeal of the plane ride, he felt thoroughly restored. The discomfort of the stabbing in Washington had left him. His problem right now was breakfast. He could have eaten a polar bear roasted over a spit.

He lit the stove again and this time read Schmidt's instructions. The mug that sat on top could be filled with small packages included in the fare. They were Schmidt's own gourmet meals, in miniature, all able to fit into the oversize mug and be cooked in their own plastic bags.

When his stomach was satisfied, Carter unzipped the tent and scooped snow away from the front. The two duffel bags were still there, some of their goodies as yet unexamined. Carter's weapons were still in the bags, including two deadly gas bombs that he taped to his inner thigh. He'd thought about taping them just inside his parka, but old habits die hard. They would be concealed where hundreds of searchers had not discovered them over the years.

Carter examined his clothes. He put on a skintight black outfit that would have done a second-story man proud. Over this he climbed into the uniform of the Inspector General's Major Anatoly Marchenko. And over all this, he donned the down parka and snowmobile pants.

So what was he to do hundreds of miles from nowhere? The only compensation he had was his own anonymity.

He went through Schmidt's goods again and came across a box he hadn't examined before. It was a miniature compass on top and a sextant on the bottom. Carter spread an empty duffel bag on the snow, spread out the topographical map Schmidt had provided, and using the sextant, plotted his exact position. According to the scale on the Silva compass, he was only five miles from the coastal town of Guba. He took a bearing on the town, cleaned up the camp, and started out for Guba using the awkward snowshoe gait he'd learned earlier.

Every five minutes he took a sighting with his compass. He was in a sea of white. The snow was coming down in a light powder. He could see nothing but the tracks he'd made.

It took almost six hours to make the five miles, but he finally came to the outskirts of town. The first thing he was aware of was the barking of dogs. They weren't barking at him. They were secured to a sleigh and had been left waiting while their master visited in a low-slung hut.

The town was no more than a village. It would be

Eskimo, probably Inuit this close to the Bering Sea. Even here they should have a garrison and some equipment.

He spotted it without difficulty. A lone guard was posted outside a hut that was about twenty feet square. The Killmaster took off his snowshoes and secured them in a sling on his back. The snow had been packed to a hard base in the town. In his multiple layers of clothing he tested Hugo's release and was satisfied.

First he needed a slow recon of the town without being seen. A circle of the whole town took only five minutes. The smell of wood burning brought back memories of friendlier campfires. The object of his recon was parked behind the military shack, an industrial strength snow machine with skis in front and oversize twin tractors in back. It was large enough to satisfy his needs, but it had a trailer attached that would take time to disconnect.

Carter thought his plan through before making his move. He was at the back of the shack. It had three small windows, but they were completely frozen over. God, what a way to live, he thought as he approached the guard, trying not to let his boots crunch in the fresh snow.

The guard's vision was impaired by the size of his parka. He was turning to challenge the noise of crunching snow, his Kalashnikov at the ready, when the stiletto blade entered his side and punctured his heart. He stood still for a moment, his chest cavity flooding, then his knees started to sag and he went down, Carter easing him into the white carpet.

The Killmaster reached for Pierre, tore him from skin that was turning blue in the process, and opened the barracks door.

Four men occupied the hut. Two were in bunks, totally immobile. One was at a stove pouring coffee into a mug. A third sat at a table playing a solitary game of cards.

All eyes shifted to him, eyes that held no suspicion, only curiosity. Carter twisted the halves of Pierre, tossed it into the cabin, and bolted the door from the outside.

One burst of an AK-47 tore at the door over his head as he flopped to his belly. But the action was fast and ended quickly. No one survived the small bomb if they weren't expecting it. This was one of the few times he felt regret for the men inside, but they were the local military, the only ones who could have stopped him.

He moved to the back of the shack and examined the snow machine. The keys were not in it. He checked the gas tank. It was full. Several fifty-gallon drums of fuel stood nearby, half covered with snow, and it took him a few minutes to wrestle them into the sled.

He brushed off the machine, then moved back to the shack. By this time several of the locals were starting to move toward the shack. He picked up the automatic rifle of the fallen guard and waved off the locals. They moved slowly, so he hurried them along with a string of 7.62mm slugs at their feet.

The Killmaster took a deep breath and entered the cabin. The key was in the most obvious place possible, hanging from a nail on the inside of the door. The four men were dead. The one at the table had tried to blast the door. He had two grenades in his webbing. Carter put them in a pocket, disabled the radio, and headed for the snowmobile.

The battery was new. The machine turned over slowly but caught within seconds. Carter made a slow circle of the town again to make sure his snowshoe tracks were covered. The natives stayed indoors. Two smaller machines stood side by side at the rear of the largest hut, obviously the local meeting place.

The machines were undoubtedly the most valuable

items the locals had ever owned. Their livelihood probably depended on them. But Carter had to weigh the harm to these civilians against the lives of more than a hundred American kids. He pulled the pin on one of the grenades and blew both machines into piles of scrap.

Something he'd seen nagged at him, and he was reluctant to leave without checking it out. An antenna. One of the huts had a shortwave antenna.

The Killmaster stopped the oversize snowmobile outside the hut and entered with his Luger in his hand. A young couple cowered in one corner, covering their children with their bodies.

"I'm sorry," Carter said as he put two 9mm bullets through the radio.

As he pulled away, the dogs were barking furiously. They still had the dogs. If they used the dogs, they could report him to the authorities. He pulled the pin on the second grenade and was about to blow the dogs and the sleigh to another dimension, but his conscience deflected his aim at the last moment. He tossed the high explosive at the back of the sled, shredding the runners.

The snow was still falling, not heavily but enough to cover his tracks to some extent. He gunned the machine. It responded sluggishly with all the gasoline in back, and he backtracked to his own camp.

The tent was still there and all of his equipment. He packed quickly, filling the two duffel bags. He tossed them on the back of the machine and started on the bearing he'd charted for Kivak.

The snow was falling hard now but he didn't care. It was a cloak to hide him from his enemies. He pulled on a pair of snow goggles and blessed Schmidt again. He had warm clothing, transportation, food, and plenty of fuel. He had two hundred miles of barren tundra to cover but he was prepared for it. This was the best way to come at them. He'd be lucky to see a tree or another settlement as he headed southeast. He was making about ten miles an hour. He'd make Kivak the following night or the morning after that. They would be forewarned. It didn't matter. He could attack at any time. His people would be at Eielson Air Force Base. A carrier was probably as close as they could get one to the winter ice floes.

Maybe they would give the C-32s air cover from Eielson. He really didn't care. When the time came, he would radio in and they would come. He'd seen Hawk's face and General Farmer's. He'd seen the determination register on the countenance of the President and he knew. They'd get the kids home if they had to send an armada and start World War III.

But it was up to him now. And he was getting close.

# THIRTEEN

Yevgeny Popolov sat in his oversize swivel chair, the exact duplicate of one he'd seen in *Forbes* magazine, and fumed while he waited for Boris Ruzimatov. The office was huge. Unlike many of his predecessors, Popolov was a materialist. He had the best office, the best dacha, the best limousine, and more guards than any man since the revolution. He also had power. He had consolidated his position since his elevation to the top post ten years earlier. Most men of power in the republic were his cronies, men who followed his line to the letter.

The failure of his intelligence program was the worst blow that his regime had suffered. Had it continued, the United States, the one country he hated above all others, would have been on its knees. He would have had superbly trained agents at every level of government and industry, people born to the job. Every one, and he would have had thousands, was capable of killing in hundreds of ways. At his order, each of his people, close to the President, senators, and congressmen, would have killed them instantly in one bloody takeover and the Secret Service would have been powerless. The bomb had never worked because of the threat of retaliation. This new tactic, this total infiltration, was beyond reprisals.

The door opened and an aide ushered in Boris Ruzimatov. The ferret-faced man stood in front of Popolov's desk without a word. He was uneasy, scared for the first time in the presence of the one man in the republic that could have him killed without trial.

Popolov kept him standing. He too was silent. He made no pretense of being busy, of shuffling papers on his desk. Indeed, the desk was empty as usual. He wanted his KGB chief to squirm before he started shredding him a little at a time.

"Explain," he finally said.

"May I sit?"

"Explain," Popolov repeated, a few decibels louder.

"How can I explain? The children have disappeared from Lumumba. Pestovo has been penetrated and those candidates are also gone."

"How could they get them out?" the seated man asked. "How could they get this close to Moscow without detection?"

"That question bothers me. I don't have the answer."

Popolov's face changed from pink to a darker shade, almost red. "Bothers you? *Bothers* you? It had better bother you, comrade. Does it mean that they could land in Moscow undetected?"

"No, First Minister."

"No? How can you be sure, Ruzimatov? After this, how can you be sure of anything?"

Ruzimatov, usually a voluble man, sat silent. Nothing had shaken him as had the raid on Pestovo. It was impregnable, less than two hundred miles from where he stood, guarded by the best men the Soviet Union had been able to produce.

"What are the Americans up to now? Are they mustering an attack force? What?"

"We have no intelligence to suggest such action. The cloud cover over their territory has made satellite coverage almost impossible."

"I'm told they have cameras that can observe us through cloud cover. Why are we always behind them?" The big man moved from his desk and began to pace the huge office.

Ruzimatov turned to follow him, his stomach tied in knots. He had never been subject to criticism since joining the party. His record had always been beyond reproach. "That is not my department, First Minister."

"Not your department. I'm hearing that more and more often from my ministers lately. Maybe they are too complacent, Ruzimatov. Maybe I should have you do some house cleaning. Then you can sit in your office on Dzerzhinsky Square and wait for your fate, comrade." He moved back to his desk and picked up the red telephone. "Now, get the hell out of my sight," he said before anyone answered at the other end.

The phone rang four times and the red light on the wall next to the President flashed incessantly before he reached for it. The call had been unexpected. The phone was to be used only under the most critical conditions.

General Farmer, the CJCS, was sitting opposite him. They had been discussing the strategy at Chukchi. The C-325 were in the air carrying the Delta people. They were being refueled constantly by tankers. Three extra squadrons of F-16s had been flown in from southern bases. The carrier *Ticonderoga* was at the edge of the

ice floe south of Alaska and her F-14 Tomcats were on
Red Alert. They put out the word to the intelligence
community that they were having war games exercises
in concert with the Canadians. To make the ruse realistic,
the Canadians had sent ground troops to the western
Yukon. They formed up two battalions along the border
with Alaska, arctic troops, and they made no secret of
their presence.

The President of the United States answered, his voice
unwavering.

"Yevgeny Popolov," the man in Moscow said, spit-
ting out his name without the usual pleasantries. "You
have committed grave acts of aggression within my country. I have instructed my people to go on Yellow Alert."

"A waste of time, Popolov," the President said, his
voice equally tinged with venom. "Your people have
been committing the most vile acts imaginable against
the citizens of my country. No crime could be worse
than stealing our children."

"That is a lie! We have stolen no children," Popolov
replied, his English adequate but heavily accented. "And
I demand to know why twenty of my people, all suspected
subversives, spent two days in your embassy."

The President had pressed a button that activated a
speakerphone so the general could hear. He put his mouth
over the speaker and raised his shoulders, looking for
the best answer.

"Tell him they learned of the plot and we kidnapped
them temporarily to give our people time to get the kids
out of the country. Tell him our kids are home and already
under intense interrogation. We have learned a great deal
about the whole operation and threaten to release the
details to the international press."

General Farmer had not been elevated to CJCS as a

matter of seniority. He earned his advancement every step of the way. He'd been in charge of G2, army intelligence, at one time and understood the philosophy of international intrigue as well as any man. The statements were relayed to the President without hesitation, so when he spoke once more to Popolov, the words seemed to be the thoughts he'd dredged up after only a moment's thought.

The line was silent for a few seconds. "It is reported to me that you tripled your forces in Alaska. If you try any more acts of aggression, I will not hesitate to throw all my available forces at you."

"Make my day, Yevgeny. I'm not backing down this time."

"This could be World War Three. It could be the last war fought on this planet," Popolov warned.

"I'm not easing off, Popolov. Not until every child that you have taken is returned, and I don't care what it takes," the President said, his voice like a whip. "You really stepped over the line this time and you'll never know what hit you if you go up against me."

The President slammed down the receiver and looked over at his chief of military staff who was grinning. "You know what you've done?" he asked.

"Someone has to tell them once in a while."

"Too bad you don't record everything like Nixon. I'd have given a month's pay to play that back to the next meeting of the Joint Chiefs. You'd have been their friend for life."

"But it could have been foolish, Chris. We've got a man who's trying to infiltrate Kivak and I've inflamed Popolov so badly he's likely to send half his military to defend it."

"Can't be done. He's limited up there. They can't

possibly put as much hardware into play as we can. As
for our spook, he's probably within hours of doing his
job. It's too late for Popolov to do anything but warn
them.''

"Which could be costly. Our guy could be compromised.''

"I know that man. So do you. If anyone can pull it
off, Carter can.''

"Maybe you're right. But we've just thrown up another barrier for him.''

The snow was falling steadily. Carter had refueled
several times and thrown off the excess barrels. He'd
debated disconnecting the sleigh as he came within
twenty miles but wanted to leave as little debris behind
as possible.

The going had been rough. The machine was big, old,
and clumsy. The snow had been clogging his goggles
every few minutes and he stopped frequently to clear
them.

Without warning, he came across fresh truck tracks.
The tires had thrown off packed snow to the northeast,
so it had been traveling away from the coast, heading
inland. He checked his compass again, following the
tracks he could barely see now in the blinding snow, and
realized the truck had come from Kivak and he'd been
off course by about ten degrees.

It was decision time. He had the major's uniform in
his pack and he could look as formidable as ever. If he
used it, how would he explain how he got there? They
would know every vehicle that arrived by land and air.
There was no way he could fake a recent arrival.

Reluctantly, he came to the conclusion that it was time
to hole up. He pushed the old snow machine to within

five miles of Kivak and stopped. The snow stopped falling and the sky was clear, a dark blue with stars so plentiful they covered the barren wastes with an eerie white and blue light.

He took a star shot and pinpointed his position. He was to the northwest of the town. His most strategic location would be the opposite side, closer to the Bering Sea, away from all vehicular traffic and on the other side of the airstrip.

With no difficulty now that the snow had stopped falling, he circled the town and picked a position for his camp behind a deserted knoll. He pitched his tent. The scenery was beautiful. He could smell wood smoke from the camp but could see no one. He set up the tent, parked the snow machine behind it, and prayed for snow. He wanted his tracks covered.

The material Schmidt sent to light his stove was a marvel. It gave off plenty of heat and no smoke or smell. And it obviously wasn't toxic. After a meal he cooked over the stove, he crawled to the top of his knoll and surveyed the larger knoll that was the camp.

It was a beehive of activity. Soldiers ringed the whole area and more troops were being brought in. New groupings of surface to-air missiles were being installed. If the Delta Force came in now, despite their skills, they would be shot out of the sky before they got into action. Carter unpacked his radio and was patched through to AXE headquarters within seconds. He asked for Hawk but learned that AXE's headman was in the war room at the White House. Rupert Smith came on instead.

"I've decided to lay low for a while, Smitty," he told him. "I can't go in now."

"We've had Delta Force in the air for ten hours. We'll

have to pull them back. You know the kind of treatment they've had. They'll be pissed.''

He had to keep the message short. "Can't be helped, Smitty. We've got to sit it out and wait for the best conditions. Tell Crunch Ballard not to get discouraged. We'll get the bastards.''

He signed off and waited for an hour before he tuned into the satellite again and checked out the weather. An arctic cold front was moving across Chuckchi and would paralyze Alaska for the next few days. Was this good or bad? It had to be good for him. The enemy would be pinned down by minus-one-hundred-degree weather. Deep, biting cold could be debilitating to the best troops in the world. The Delta boys would sit idle in warm barracks at Eielson while the Soviets froze their asses off, constantly on the alert.

It began to snow again before the cold front, led by a massive high-pressure area, moved silently over them. Snow had covered his camp. He crawled inside the tent, fed the stove and turned it to a low setting, then curled up in a down bag and fell asleep in seconds.

Colonel Ballard had been given the courtesy of the officers' mess at Eielson Air Force Base. He sat with his officers and listened to their gripes.

"Another bullshit mission. I knew it was too good to be true," one of the lieutenants said. He'd been alerted and canceled so many times he was dizzy from the effect. Like the other men, he'd been dedicated, had honed his skills to the max, and still he sat on his butt on the sidelines.

"This stinks. Why don't they just scrub the whole mission and get us the hell back home?" another chimed in.

The last one to speak was a captain in his early forties. He'd been with Charlie Beckwith through the tough years of forming Delta Force. He'd been with the group that aborted at Iran. He was also a man the others listened to because he'd earned their respect the hard way, on the ground, on his belly, crawling under the barbed wire with the lowliest of them. "I say we take it easy. I've got a feeling about this one. Hey, at least it's different scenery, right? Anyone want to go back to North Carolina and sit on his ass there again? Whaddayah say, Crunch?"

Colonel Crunch Ballard liked the captain. If his bones weren't so old, he'd trade every man in Delta for clones of that one. He looked across the table at him and smiled, then his face took on a more serious expression.

"You ever see a man sit across from you with eyes that were like brown agates, hard and cold? You ever talk to a man who looked at you and you knew right away he could do what he said? And I mean *anything he said*?"

He waited for a reaction. No one spoke. They were hanging on every word.

"I met a guy like that in Smoky Camp. He came to me and asked me to do this job. Then you know what he did?"

"What did he do, Crunch?" the lieutenant asked, taking advantage of the forced intimacy.

"He went into Moscow posing as a Russian major and he pulled twenty of our kids right out from under their noses, kids they'd kidnapped, kids they planned to train and use against us. The kids are in Washington right now being debriefed."

They sat in silence, some raising their cans of Coors to their mouths, their attention riveted on their commander.

"Did the guy come home and visit the President and have him pin on a medal? No way. This is a different kind of guy," he said, looking around the table at them, looking straight into their eyes, holding their attention. "He traveled to a Spetsnaz camp only a hundred and forty miles from Moscow and he rescued another seventy of our kids. *Our* kids! *American* kids!"

"How the hell could he get them out?" a major asked.

"This guy's boss has so much clout, he talks the CJCS into using our first three operational B-2 Stealth bombers. They slipped in quiet as hell and picked them up," Ballard went on, knowing they would not spread the word beyond the Delta group. "Somehow, the guy drugged the whole Spetsnaz camp and the personnel at the air base by putting something in their drinking water. The ones who stayed conscious he kills himself, using their own weapons."

"Jesus!" was the only word that followed his speech. It came from the brash young lieutenant.

"You know where this guy is now, while we're sitting here in this warm mess drinking cold beer?" Ballard asked.

No one was about to speak now, nor were they about to miss one word of his story. "I'm not sure where he is, not exactly, but I'll give you a scenario that fits from what I know of him.

"He's holed up in a tent close to the base we got to take out. He knows it's too hot to take out now, and who the hell would know better than him? He's keeping the place under surveillance. He knows we're in for one hell of a few days of arctic weather, so he's going to sit it out in his goddamned tent and he's asking us to play along.

"That crazy bastard's got to destroy their ground-to-air missile installations or we're dead before we hit the ground. He's got to get inside a fortified underground city alone, set charges, warn the occupants to get out or be killed, then he's got to get out and hope we don't shoot him in the process.''

He waited while they came out of the state of shock he'd created.

''What will the guy look like?'' the lieutenant asked, his tone entirely subdued.

''Okay. You've been briefed that the Spetsnaz will be in camouflaged battle dress. The kids we want will be in green uniforms. My guess is this guy will be in black. Now that's a guess, but it makes sense,'' Ballard told them, lifting his beer can to his mouth, draining it, and crushing it in one powerful hand.

''We pass the word that this guy's got to be handled like pure gold,'' the lieutenant said, as if talking to himself.

''Now you've got it,'' Ballard said, going along with the sentiment. ''After the spell in his tent and the action he's gone through, we'd damn sure better bring him home.''

''We could use a guy like that,'' one of the captains said.

Ballard looked at him and at the others and shook his head. ''There's only one guy like that, you useless bastards,'' he said, smiling at them, the men he'd trained and come to think of as family. ''And he's doing a solo job. Just thank whoever you pray to that you never have to live like that.''

# FOURTEEN

As the days passed, Carter crawled to his observation post a half-dozen times. Gradually the tension at the camp seemed to ease. Fewer guards were on duty at the entrance; only one man was posted at each battery of SAM-like missiles. The traffic from outside slowed to a crawl. He decided it was time to make his move.

In the Kremlin, Yevgeny Popolov sat at his massive desk alone. He had called Kivak twice a day and checked with his military advisers almost hourly. The Americans were not making a move. The aircraft carrier had not left the scene and he could get no intelligence on Eielson, but everything seemed quiet.

He was by nature a skeptical man but after a week he could hold back his elation no longer. He called in Boris Ruzimatov and his most trusted advisors. He played them a tape of his talk with the American President with simultaneous translation. He ordered up a tray of drinks and they all toasted his success. The Americans were gutless. Popolov had pushed them to the wall and won.

"I want our agents in the northwest United States replaced," Popolov said. "I want Lumumba in operation as soon as you can deliver candidates. We will build Pestovo as an impregnable fortress," he gloated as he waved his glass in the air, spilling the potent liquid on the polished surface of his desk. "We've won."

Carter reached for the radio in one of the duffel bags and tuned in to the satellite used by AXE. He ran the dial to the correct frequency and was answered by the simulated voice. "Release the dogs," he said. "Tell Hawk that N3 is going in now."

At Eielson, Ballard was sitting with some of his Delta men at the table in the officers' mess they'd adopted as their own. The time for drinking had long since passed. They'd been on maneuvers in the arctic cold every day, but never strayed more than a couple of miles from the base. One of their men was posted to shoot a star shell if they got the go sign.

Their enthusiasm had waned. A week of waiting, knowing they could be called any minute or told to stand down, was wearing on the nerves.

Gradually they were aware of the noise level of the base picking up. Lights flooded the tarmac at eleven at night. Jets were towed from bunkers and fired up. Their C-32s were revved, the hatches open and inviting. While their anticipation started to climb and they got to their feet, their officer of the day came charging in, his face flushed. Snow fell from his clothes and melted flakes dripped from his fur-lined parka.

*"It's a go!"* he shouted.

• • •

Carter turned the duffel bags inside out and checked over everything Schmidt had provided. The man was a wonder at thinking of everything. He had a dozen small plastique bombs, primed, radio operated, each no larger than a cigarette lighter, but powerful enough to blow a troop carrier off a road. Carter tuned them all to the same frequency and synchronized the equally small mechanism that would blow them. He packed them into his oversize right patch pocket and continued his preparations.

In his left pocket he stored a half-dozen similar bombs he'd set at a different frequency. He placed the transmitter for the dozen in his right pocket in the breast pocket above them and did the same on his left side. He had his own weapons in place, a fact that gave him confidence regardless of any other weapons he might have.

One of the last items he examined was a long, slim box. He opened it to find a rifle no larger than a boy's air rifle. It was Howard Schmidt's own design for a compressed air gun. Twenty small darts were lined up in the inner lining of the case. He carefully punched the points through the webbing around his waist and he was almost ready. The last item was a gun to fire a star shell.

He had to use the plastic snowshoes he'd come to rely on for trips back and forth between his tent and his observation post. They were surprisingly resilient in that bitter cold but like all snowshoes they were noisy. Fortunately, with the rifle, he didn't have to close in and rely on Hugo.

It was snowing, not the huge flakes he'd fought through on the way here or the light powder of other days, but something in between, slow and constant as if they were being doled out by a precise machine somewhere above him.

The missile installations ringed the camp, a dozen of

them, each a couple of hundred feet from the other. Carter walked awkwardly toward the closest, knelt, and brought up the rifle. He had to jackknife it to set the air pressure and slip one of the darts down the barrel. It was primitive. He hoped it would be effective.

Without previous experience with the piece, Carter allowed a foot of drop for the dart. He aimed almost a foot above the guard's head and saw him go down.

He trudged to the outpost. The dart had penetrated the man's outer clothing and taken him in the neck between his body armor and steel helmet. Carter slipped a bomb from his right pocket and tossed it into an opening between the four missiles that were pointed skyward on a revolving base.

How long would the dart put the man out? Schmidt hadn't left instructions. He slipped Hugo from his sheath, then decided that Schmidt must have allowed him a couple of hours. If he didn't believe that, he'd have to slit the throats of a dozen or more unconscious men. No matter how often a man like Carter faced a kill, it was not easy. It was worse when it was wholesale slaughter. He slipped Hugo back into his sheath and went on to the next man.

They were crossing over the shore of enemy territory for the first time. Two squadrons of F-16 fighters were at twenty thousand feet and on Soviet radar. They could see a similar number of MiG fighters on their radar about a hundred miles to the west. They were both closing at about a thousand miles an hour. The pilots were nervous. None had encountered a Soviet MiG and they knew the new Foxbats, the MiG32, was almost the equal of their F-16s.

On the scope they could see at least a hundred planes

on their tail. They'd had brief radio contact with them—
navy F-14 Tomcats—their pilots convinced they were
the equal of the F-16.

Nothing of the lumbering C-32s showed up on their
radar. In the time it took to check their instruments for
the last time, the Foxbats had screamed past them a
thousand feet higher in the sky and were turning to zero
in at missile range.

As he finished with the last of the missile launchers,
Carter could hear the fighters overhead. He had little
time to waste. He pulled off the snowshoes and trudged
toward the front entrance with the parka of one of the
guards draped over his head and shoulders. Twenty feet
from the opening to the underground town, Carter pulled
off his webbing and put the two high-explosive transmitters into waterproof containers. He hid the webbing
in the snow not far from the door.

It had all been easy up to this point. If the darts were
effective, the guards wouldn't give him trouble. The
difficult part was yet to come. He walked up to the first
guard and asked him for a light.

"No smoking on duty, comrade. You know that," the
professional soldier chastised, a huge man who out-
weighed Carter by fifty pounds.

But the man from AXE wasn't interested in a smoke.
Hugo was in his hand and entered the man's throat just
above his flack jacket. He had to hold the man up as the
Soviet dropped his weapon and his knees buckled. Blood
poured from his throat in a constant stream, covering the
knife. Carter had to keep to one side a few seconds for
the guard's chest cavity to fill with blood and for him to
lose consciousness.

The Killmaster tried to prop the guard into position

against the side of the huge entrance doors but could not. It didn't really matter. The whole area was covered with blood.

Carter crossed to the other side of the doors and caught a guard going the other way. He circled his hand around the man's throat, letting the stiletto do its job. This time he let the man lay where he fell. His arm was soaked in blood, so he pulled off the bloodstained parka and tossed it to one side.

Now the Killmaster was dressed all in black again. He flipped the lock on the small door that was part of the massive gates and stepped inside. The court was poorly lighted. He found a small room to apply black makeup to his face, then moved from shadow to shadow, trying to avoid contact as he carefully placed the bombs he'd reserved to destroy the city.

One task remained. He had to find their communications center and broadcast a message to evacuate, a message that would panic the occupants into a mad scramble for the door. That was the plan.

The underground town was laid out like a huge office building. There was way he could find the communications room without help. Groups of trainees moved from room to room, from level to level. Spetsnaz, battle-tested brutes complete with their full load of armament, moved about purposefully. He managed to avoid them all in the dimly lit corridors.

Then he found it. On a corridor wall, a directory told him exactly where he was and how to find his way. He memorized the chart, including every room number and every level. The communications room was numbered 303, presumably on the third level below ground. He was standing between rooms 120 and 121 on the top level. He had the option of using stairwells or elevators.

Carter had just decided on the stairs close by when something heavy and solid hit the side of his head and he went down. The last thing he remembered was looking at the leather laces of a pair of Spetsnaz boots.

"On your tail!" a wing man screamed at his leader. "Break off! Break off!"

"To hell! I'm locked on! You get the bastard!"

The squadron leader, ignoring the bogey on his tail, watched his missile disintegrate the MiG he'd been chasing, then pulled up in a vertical climb. The chasing MiG tried to follow but was short by a fraction of a second and the wing man was on him like a leech. He too watched as his missile smoked through the distance between them and, maintaining contact with its exhaust heat, streaked up the bandit's tail.

In the lead C-32, Ballard called to the base for instructions.

"Circle at three thousand. Fighters at twenty thousand giving you cover."

"What's the score?" he asked.

"That's classified, Colonel."

"Don't be an asshole. What's the fucking score?"

"This is General Farmer, Ballard," the familiar voice of the CJCS broke in. "You have a full umbrella. We've lost one Tomcat and one of our boys from Eielson. They're outgunned two to one. The score is seven MiGs to two of ours. Now stay the hell off the air."

"Yes, sir," he complied. He punched a button on the intercom and called to his troops. "The score upstairs is seven to two for the good guys. Keep your cool. We'll get our go sign soon. That's a promise."

He turned off the intercom and sat motionless for a

moment. He wasn't at all sure that he could keep his promise.

Carter opened his eyes and as soon as he was fully conscious, he knew that he had one of the worst headaches he could remember. He was tied to a chair, naked, his clothes tossed in a corner. Two colonels were standing over him. Their faces registered the triumph that would bring them honor and promotion.

"I am Colonel Nikolai Leonid Simolin and my colleague is Colonel Igor Victor Sobolev," the taller of the two announced in Russian. He was dressed immaculately in a blue uniform with the red and gold shoulder boards of a full colonel. The other, a junior in the ranks of newly commissioned colonels, was at least five years younger and three inches shorter.

"And you are the famous Killmaster. We know all about you, Nick Carter," he announced, his expression reflecting his triumph. "I am in charge of the whole exchange program. With the loss of Lumumba and Pestovo I was about to face ruin. Then you turn up at my doorstep. Thank you, Carter. You've saved the project and you've saved my life."

Two Spetsnaz guards stood at attention at the door. The room was equipped for various forms of interrogation, mostly physical. He had to get out and fast. The Delta boys would be overhead. The fighter jocks would be in the thick of it. He couldn't let it fail now. He had only minutes.

"You, Colonel, are an asshole," he announced, hawking up a glob of spit and aiming it at the overconfident officer.

Simolin went crazy. "Tie him to the rack! Give him

a dozen lashes! We'll make the bastard sorry he was born!'' he barked at them.

The two soldiers moved like robots, untied his hands, and turned him toward the back wall and the hardwood rack.

Carter tried to break loose but was held fast. He was tied to the rack, his toes barely touching the floor, his wrists held by Inuit rawhide.

The lash struck without warning, flaying skin from his back. It had been unexpected and he cried out. The lash descended again and this time he was prepared and took the blow without flinching.

"Turn him around! I want to see his face,'' Simolin said.

The guards had one of Carter's hands free when they spotted the small gas bomb. One reached for it, but Carter caught him on the chin with a knee. The other guard kneed him in the kidney and he swung from the rawhide that still captured the other wrist.

Simolin and Sobolev started to draw their pistols but decided to take him by hand instead. That was their fatal mistake. Carter had been deep breathing for the past few seconds. Now he inhaled deeply, tore the gas bomb loose with his free hand, and was able to open it as they came at him.

He hung by one wrist, his toes barely touching the floor, and watched them die. He could hold his breath for four minutes, but this time he knew the four minutes would not be enough.

The Spetsnaz warrior lay at his feet. Carter moved to stand on him and give himself some relief. A minute had passed.

The man's commando knife was under him, but there was no way Carter could get to it. The spring-loaded knife was close to Carter's toes. The trigger was accessible. But how could he aim it? he wondered.

Christ! It was all he had. He maneuvered the man's body with his feet until he thought the knife was pointed at his wrist and moved a toe to the trigger.

Two minutes. What were the odds? He flicked the trigger with his big toe and heard the knife let go. It was so fast he didn't feel the pain, but he was free and fell on top of the dead man.

Two and a half minutes. He looked at his wrist and saw the long shallow cut. No major arteries severed.

Three minutes. His clothes. He pulled them on in seconds and rushed out the door into the powerful arms of a Spetsnaz. The man wasn't expecting him. Carter grabbed for the soldier's commando model AK-47 and pushed the man into the room, keeping the gun for himself. He held the door from the outside until he felt no resistance.

How long had he been out of action? His luck had been running well until then. He looked at the room number on the door. It was number 313. Good. The communications room was only a few doors away.

A small man in civilian clothes looked up as he entered. He had to be KGB. The bastards were everywhere. The agent went for his gun but Carter tore him in half with the Kalashnikov before he could reach it.

A switch was flipped. Carter recognized the Soviet symbols for broadcast. But in the second it took for him to assimilate, another agent entered, unarmed, and kicked him in the groin.

Carter fell back in pain, but he forced himself to react normally and Wilhelmina put a hole in the man's temple before he could react.

The control panel was a mass of sticky blood and brain

matter. Carter pushed the agent aside and grabbed for the mike. He flipped the talk switch on the mike and used his best Russian to issue the warning.

ATTENTION. ATTENTION. THIS MESSAGE WILL NOT BE REPEATED. A SABOTEUR HAS INFILTRATED THE COMPLEX. TIMED EXPLOSIVES ARE SET TO DETONATE IN TEN MINUTES.

PROCEED TO THE EXIT IN AN ORDERLY MANNER. WE ALL HAVE PLENTY OF TIME. DO NOT PANIC. END OF MESSAGE.

He could hear them all move around him, and when he left the room, he was part of a human chain that took to the stairs and didn't stop until they were outside and ringing the missile sites. Carter estimated the subjects at about a hundred and twenty, the guards at about fifty.

The Killmaster peeled off at the door and searched for his webbing. He found the webbing and strapped it on. By this time he was in a mixed costume. His black pants and boots stuck out below the Spetsnaz parka. If everyone wasn't in a panic, they'd have spotted that he was different.

He moved away from the missile sites. Everyone was clear of the building and the launching pads. Carter sought the cover of an old supply truck and pulled out the transmitters. He forgot which was which. To hell with it. It didn't really matter.

He pulled out an antenna and flipped on a switch. A red light glowed. Without wasting time, he pushed the button and the top of the installation blew like a volcano erupting. Debris was falling everywhere when Carter pulled out the other transmitter and readied it for its job.

"Who the hell are you?" a Spetsnaz asked, standing behind him, his gun held loosely in one hand.

Carter whirled and his Luger barked before the man could blink. This was no time to be concerned with finesse. He flipped the switch, pressed the button, and all twelve missile installations blew sky-high.

It was a sight that everyone there would remember. The missile launchers churned their steel burdens into the air. They came down as scraps of twisted metal, the fins of the missiles twisted but their warheads intact.

The explosions ripping through the blasted city were so spectacular that everyone moved back a few feet and stood, their eyes glued to the night sky.

Carter fired the star shell and raced for the protection of a twisted metal hulk that had once been a missile site.

The choppers came in on cue. Three of them, apparently newer versions of the old Hueys, hovered at five hundred feet and dropped their cluster bombs.

They were right on the money. Thousands of small darts fanned out in a circle encompassing the whole installation. Carter could see the whole action. All the candidates went down and all the incidental personnel. The Spetsnaz were protected by body armor and steel helmets. Few of them went down. They took cover behind anything they could find.

Carter felt a slight pricking in his ankle. He looked down and saw one of the darts. Damn! He'd been through all this and was going to be left behind. He was in a Spetsnaz parka. Before darkness claimed him, he rolled over on his back and tried to get out of the parka, but he felt the darkness close around him again before he could get the offending garment away from his body.

• • •

The Delta Force men were out of their aircraft before their wheels stopped turning. They came in low and firing. They knew their targets and picked off Spetsnaz with deadly accuracy. If a soldier of the Soviet showed an inch of skin, a bullet found it. Body armor made no difference. Most of the Americans carried the Hecker and Koch MP5 9mm parabellum submachine gun. Lighter and with a better feel than the Thomson MG and with more versatility than the CAR-15s or M-16s, the Delta Force had adopted it and had fired thousands of rounds with it. With their H&Ks set at three-round bursts, they came on in waves, using anything available for cover, and hit the Soviet elite with the most deadly rain of fire that was possible.

But this was what they'd trained for over a period of years. While the Spetsnaz bayonetted human wretches, the Delta men learned to raid terrorist-held positions, hostages and all, and differentiate between friend and foe in a split second. Even under pressure, they could shoot the center out of a quarter at fifty feet.

Crunch Ballard was one of the men in the front rank. He carried no insignia, as was the custom in his specialized business. He took out his targets as did all his men, then made a sweep of the whole area.

"Are they all down?" he asked his major.

"Every one."

"Coup de grace?"

"In progress, sir."

"Then get the kids on board as fast as you can. Some of our guys can carry two. Get moving!"

Ballard made a complete sweep again and couldn't find Carter. They were all back in the C-32s. The kids were all dumped in any which way, like loose duffel bags. They had counted 121 of them.

"Where the hell is Carter?" Ballard asked.

"No one saw him," the major responded.

"We've got to get the hell out," Ballard said. "Volunteers for one more sweep?" he called out.

Every Delta man on the plane jumped to his side. "Okay. Tell the other ships to get the hell out. We meet back here in two minutes. If you're not here in two minutes, we're gone," he said, taking off at a dead run.

They spread out and examined every body on the ground. The young lieutenant, the last man to be accepted into their officer ranks, pulled the parka from Carter's face and noticed the black outfit. "Here, Colonel!" he called out.

Ballard was on him in five seconds. He took one look at Carter and breathed a sigh of relief. No hole in his head like the others—no coup de grace as he'd ordered. A miracle. The big man scooped him up like a sack of flour and ran for the airplane with seconds to spare.

With the wheels turning, he shouted, "Anyone missing?"

"No, sir," the major reported.

"Wounded?"

"Five, sir. None critical."

He stood, regardless of the speed of takeoff and hung on to the webbing that ringed the fuselage. *"We did it, you bastards! We beat the fucking Spetsnaz on their own ground!"*

A roar sounded throughout the aircraft as he sat. He thought about the years he'd been frustrated, the years he'd not been able to prove they had the right stuff, the goddamned *best* stuff.

· · ·

A medic shoved an ammonia capsule under Carter's nose and he came around, barely. "My balls hurt," he said.

Ballard and those around him laughed. "That's it? Your balls hurt?"

"Got kicked in the balls."

A hundred pairs of eyes looked at him with admiration. Every fighting man on the plane was the best any country could produce, but they knew they'd never match the daring and skill of this one.

"What about casualties?" Carter asked, sitting up, rubbing his head.

"I have a dozen wounded altogether, none serious. We lost two Tomcats and an F-16," Ballard said.

"Shit. Six good men. Six families back home who've got to be told," Carter mumbled.

"We salvaged a hundred and twenty-one kids here. How many at the other places?" Ballard asked.

"Let's see," Carter said, almost falling under the effect of the drug again. "Twenty at Lumumba. Seventy-six at Pestovo."

"That's two hundred and seventeen," Ballard said. "The President should be happy about that kind of trade-off."

"You don't know him, then," Carter said, almost asleep again. "The guy in the White House will lay awake all night thinking about the families of the dead flyboys. That's the way . . . way he is," he said as his eyes closed.

"And what kind of guy are you?" Ballard asked softly, out of the earshot of the others. He pulled a blanket around the sleeping man, his face one broad smile. "What the hell kind of guy are you?"

# DON'T MISS THE NEXT NEW NICK CARTER SPY THRILLER

## *DRAGON SLAY*

"Who are you?"

"My name is Nick Carter." He crossed the room and flipped open his credentials case. "I'm with a special unit of the State Department."

"The kidnap unit?" she hissed, and mashed out the cigarette she had been puffing wildly but not inhaling.

"Not exactly," Carter replied dryly. "My apologies for what has happened to you and your friend. It couldn't be helped."

"The hell you say. Where is Rhoda?"

"On another floor. I'm afraid she tried to use a pair of scissors on one of the attendants."

"Good for her."

"She had to be sedated."

"Where am I and what the hell is going on?"

Carter took a deep breath and dived in. "I'm afraid you have stumbled onto something that involves national security."

"I sure have," she barked, her voice going up a full two octaves. "The question is, whose national security?

Does our State Department work for the Red Chinese now?''

Carter passed a hand over his eyes. "In a way, yes, we do.''

That quieted her for a moment. "What?''

"Miss Greer, you were meant to find the body of Yang Lee Yong. You were also fed clues to Yong's involvement in the smuggling of drugs. But drugs play only a minor part in it all.''

"I'm listening. Who supposedly steered me in this direction?''

"A man by the name of Sim, Dr. Chiang Sim.''

For the next half hour, Carter laid out Sim's plan to her. He held nothing back, in the hope that she would realize that the story he was offering her was better than the one she already had.

By the time he finished, an inscrutable smile crinkled her green eyes. "So you're going to waltz onto this Yatsu Island, get Sim's files, and botch up his grand plan?''

Carter nodded. "That's the idea.''

"And what happens to Sim?''

Carter hesitated. "I won't know that until the time comes." He couldn't very well tell a civilian that, if he could, he planned on terminating the good doctor.

Christie stood and began to pace. Carter lit a cigarette, watched her, and waited. He couldn't help but think that even in the sacklike hospital gown, gaping slightly open in the rear, that she was a lot of woman.

She was indeed a large woman, but the beautiful proportions of her body were in perfect relation to her size. Added to that was a face that could get you run over turning around to look at again, plus the striking hair that hung in soft waves well below her broad shoulders. A color, he found himself thinking with amusement, that would probably match exactly the downy cushion he pictured between her lithe, golden thighs.

Christie paused in her pacing and turned to face him. "You're going to do all this by yourself?"

"Pretty much so," he said nodding slowly.

"From the appearance of your head and face," she said, looking him over critically, "you should take some lessons in the art of self-defense."

Carter didn't bother with a reply. He only smiled.

"Yeah," she continued, "I should see the other guy, right?"

He stood. "Do we have a deal?"

"What happens to me while you go off to this island and play cowboy?"

"You stay here."

"No way."

He shrugged. "I'm afraid it has to be that way."

Suddenly she was a dervish. She spun, lightning fast. One kick caught him in the ribs; a second hit dead center in his gut.

The breath whistled out of his lungs and he hit the wall. He gasped but no air would come. Suddenly she was on him, moving with incredible speed. When she was a few feet from him she leaped into the air, spreading her arms and legs wide toward him, clamping them around him as their bodies thudded together.

"Ha!"

It was a yell of triumph, for now she had the hold she wanted. Her long legs wrapped around him, gripping his hips in a parody of sex, her feet interlocked behind him. Supporting their combined weight was as much as he could manage, and for a moment his coolness deserted him and he began to flail punches at her, but because she was molding herself so tightly to him he could get no power into the blows.

She ignored the fists, stretching her arms out on either side of his head and interlocking the fingers as she pulled inward. Realization of what she was going to do made him renew the struggle with added intensity.

This lady wasn't fooling around. She knew the pressure points that would put him out, and she meant to use them.

Strength was draining from him every second. Stars began to shoot across his vision as his tortured lungs labored in vain. Another few moments and he would be on his knees, then on his back.

His groping fingers closed in her hair and he tried to drag her head back, desperate for anything that would give him a moment to draw in fresh breath.

Her weight was forcing him backward, but he made one last blind effort, staggering a step forward, then flinging himself down. As her back crashed to the floor, she let out her breath in a grunt, her grip loosening for a split second. It was enough.

Carter gulped in air and even as he did so, he buried his fist, wrist deep, in her belly.

Christie was sagging but trying to rise when an enormous Chinese woman and two orderlies burst into the room. In no time they had Christie on the bed and the big Chinese woman was giving her an injection. When it was done, she turned to face Carter with a smile.

"She very tough lady."

"Yeah," Carter said, running a hand over his side to make sure his ribs were still whole. "Very tough. Keep her sedated."

The big woman nodded and Carter hit the hall. Myang was waiting for him.

"What happened to you?"

"Never mind. Let's go back to your place. I'll stay there tonight. I don't want to run around in the Lotus if they have it spotted."

She followed him to her car. "I've been thinking about that. If Sim knows about you, why even go to Taipei? Why not go right to Yatsu Island?"

"Because I want to show myself enough so that Sim's people think I'm still running around on Taiwan when I hit Yatsu. Understand?"

Myang blinked and then shook her head. "Inscrutable, you Caucasians."

—From DRAGON SLAY
A New Nick Carter Spy Thriller
From Jove in May 1990